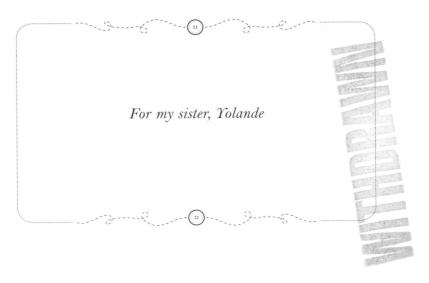

For my sister, Yolande

Beforever

Beforever is about making connections. It's about exploring the past, finding your place in the present, and thinking about the possibilities your future can bring. And it's about seeing the common thread that ties girls from all times together. The inspiring characters you will meet stand up for what they care about most: Helping others. Protecting the earth. Overcoming injustice. Through their courageous stories, discover how staying true to your own beliefs will help make your world better today—and tomorrow.

A Journey Begins

This book is about Addy, but it's also about a girl like you who travels back in time to Addy's world of 1864. You, the reader, get to decide what happens in the story. The choices you make will lead to different journeys and new discoveries.

When you reach a page in this book that asks you to make a decision, choose carefully. The decisions you make will lead to different endings. (Hint: Use a pencil to check off your choices. That way, you'll never read the same story twice.)

Want to try another ending? Read the book again—and then again. Find out what happens to you and Addy when you make different choices.

Before your journey ends, take a peek into the past, on page 180, to discover more about Addy's time.

'm staring at the page in front of me, but I still can't believe it.

I failed my social studies test. I've never failed a test before. What are my parents going to say? I know I should have studied more, but I can't keep my mind on social studies when everything's so crazy in our family.

Last year, Mom went back to school to become a teacher, so after working all day, she goes to class or a study group almost every night. Then, a month ago, Dad started a new job—and it's hundreds of miles away in another state. He can only come home one weekend a month. That's why my grandparents have moved in. They're helping around the house and taking care of my little brother and me. I love my grandparents, but everything is so different without my parents around!

Gran's driving into the school parking lot right now. I shove the test into my backpack before she pulls over. She doesn't have to know—yet.

Gran smiles and waves. "How was the test?"

Of course she remembers the test. She and Grandpa offered to help me study every night for a week.

"Um . . ." I try to stall as I get into the car.

"Was it that bad?" she asks as we drive off.

For a minute, I just stare out of the window. I've always done well in school—especially in math. I would have aced a math test, even if I hadn't studied. The thing is, I usually don't mind studying. That's because Dad sits with me at the kitchen table so that I can ask him questions. He gets me to figure out the answers on my own, but he makes it fun. I just don't feel like doing homework now that he's gone.

"It was bad, Gran," I say. "Why is it so easy to focus when I like something, and so hard when I don't?"

Gran looks at me over the top of her eyeglasses when we stop at the traffic light. "I'm sure it's hard to focus on anything when you're missing your parents so much."

I blink. "How'd you know?"

"Grandmothers know things," she says, patting my knee.

"I just don't want to disappoint Mom and Dad—especially Dad," I say as the light changes and Gran drives on. "But social studies is so boring. Who cares about all those old dates and distant places?"

"There are reasons to care," Gran says. "You know, you don't have to get an A on everything. But you do have to try your best," she scolds me gently. "Besides, doing well in school isn't just for your parents. It's for you, too."

I look at her, puzzled. "What do you mean?"

"Remember that TV program we saw?" Gran asks. "You couldn't believe that girls in some countries aren't even allowed to go to school."

I do remember. I was shocked. There's a lot I love about school: math, reading, art, seeing my friends, some of my teachers. I can't imagine not being able to go.

"You have a wonderful opportunity to learn!" Gran says. "You shouldn't waste it."

We pull into our driveway and get out of the car. My backpack feels crazy heavy, as if the bad grade is weighing it down. I don't like this feeling.

When Gran opens the kitchen door, my grandfather and little brother are eating cookies and drinking milk. Gran looks at me again. "So you'll tell your father what happened when he calls tonight? Your mom has a study group, so you can talk to her tomorrow."

"What happened?" My nosy little brother, Danny, looks wide-eyed. He's five. Gran smiles at him but doesn't answer.

Grandpa looks from me to Gran, and back at me again. "Problem?" he asks.

"I sort of didn't do well on my social studies test," I mumble. "I . . . failed it."

Grandpa looks thoughtful for a minute. "Well," he finally says, "there are consequences for every action."

"What's consequences?" Danny asks. I frown at him.

"I know you miss your dad, but he would want you to make schoolwork a priority," Grandpa says. "I think you need to focus more on your studies. So, no more after-school visits, video games, TV, or cell phone for one week. You're grounded."

I totally didn't expect this!

"But Grandpa," I say. "I finally convinced Mom to let me walk to the ice cream shop to meet Nikki and Jordan this Friday!"

Grandpa looks at Gran, but he doesn't say anything.

"Can I just please go on Friday night? I'll study every other night, and I'll do extra chores. Please

change your mind?" Am I whining? I hope not, but I see Danny rolling his eyes. "I'll even read to Danny before bed when Mom is at class."

Grandpa shakes his head. "Sweet pea, freedom and responsibility go together," he says. "You've got to work hard. You've got to show us that you're responsible enough to make good choices—like focusing on your schoolwork—in order to earn freedom. Understand?"

"Yes, Grandpa," I say. But I really don't get it. My grandparents used to be so much fun when they came to visit. Now that they live with us full-time, they're more strict. I miss Dad. I wish Mom weren't so busy. Life is so unfair!

☺ *Turn to page 6.*

I drag my two-ton backpack to my room without saying another word. I can't believe I'm going to miss Friday night with my friends! Going out on my own is a big, big deal because Mom is really protective. She always has been. Whenever we go to the mall or the grocery store, Mom points out some spot for a meeting place. If we get separated, I'm supposed to go there and wait for her to find me. But now that Dad is away, Mom is even more cautious. She drives me everywhere, even to school, which is only a few blocks away. She says, "I just want to make sure you're safe!"

Safe from what? We live in a medium-size town in Tennessee. I know everyone in our neighborhood, so it's not like I'm in a big city full of strangers. Now I even have a cell phone for emergencies. But I won't ever use it if I don't get to go anywhere.

I'm just about to start crying when Danny knocks on my door. "Gran says come help with dinner," he tells me.

We walk back to the kitchen together. "Does grounded mean you can't go anywhere?" Danny asks.

"Nowhere interesting," I say with a shrug.

Despite my glum mood, I have to admit that our

kitchen smells fantastic. Grandpa is a great cook, and everything he makes tastes wonderful, even food we've never heard of before. He and Gran are making dinner together. They remind me of my parents.

When Dad worked in town, he was always home in time to start cooking dinner. Then Mom would come in, kick off her shoes, and join him. Dad always called me the chef's assistant. I'd wash veggies while Mom and Dad moved around the stove as if they were dancing. Even Danny helped shake up the salad dressing. Dad always had a funny story to tell, and Mom would ask me about my day at school.

Remembering our good times somehow doesn't make me feel very happy. Something's not right, and it's not just the social studies test. It's the fact that Dad's gone. I can't seem to explain how I feel to anybody. My friends think I'm acting like a baby because I miss my dad so much.

"Do you want to help make the salad?" Gran asks.

"I don't think so," I say, feeling close to tears again.

"I do!" Danny hurries to wash his hands so that he can tear the lettuce.

Gran starts slicing tomatoes. "Then you can go

ahead and set the table, please," she tells me.

With all the drama about my test, I forgot to unload the dishwasher when I got home from school. That's one of the regular chores I have to do around the house to earn my allowance. *I won't be going anywhere to spend it anyway*, I think to myself. I move in slow motion as I take plates, forks, and knives out of the dishwasher. I'm not paying any attention to the way I put things on the table.

"Oh, look what you did!" Danny shouts. Gran and Grandpa turn to me.

"What are you talking about?" I ask grumpily. Danny points at the table. I've set six places, instead of four. I included spots for Mom and Dad.

"I . . . I forgot," I mumble, grabbing the extra plates and blinking back tears.

Grandpa puts his arm around my shoulder. "They won't always be gone for dinner," he says softly. "This change is only temporary."

"Even though you're apart, you're still a strong family," Gran adds, wiping a tear from my cheek. "You're going to get through this. Keep hope in your heart."

I blink back the rest of my tears, take a deep breath, and get out the drinking glasses. Gran helps Danny carry the salad bowl to the table as I pour the milk. Everyone sits down.

"Eat up!" Grandpa says, setting a platter of delicious-looking bluefish and mashed potatoes on the table.

Fish is one of Dad's favorite meals, and mine, too, but I can only pick at the food in front of me. Tonight I can't quite enjoy it. It's not just my test grade that has me down. I know that Gran and Grandpa are family, and they love Danny and me, but this just doesn't feel like a real dinner with both Mom and Dad missing.

I'm also starting to get nervous about my call with Dad. I talk to him every night on the phone, but lately we've been Skyping on the computer. Now we can see each other. It's usually great, but since I'm not good at hiding my feelings, Dad will know right away from my face that something's wrong.

☺ *Turn to page 10.*

After dinner, Gran and I clear the dishes. I can hear Grandpa and Danny playing a game of "musical chairs without music" in the living room. Grandpa's clapping a beat while he and Danny march around the coffee table. When Grandpa stops clapping, I hear them both flop on the sofa, giggling wildly.

By the time I join them in the living room, the game is done and Grandpa has pulled out his coin collection. He brought it with him from his house—that's how much he loves these old coins. Danny seems to love them, too. He's bouncing up and down.

"History is more than just a bunch of dates!" Grandpa's saying as I curl up in a chair across from the sofa. "It's about real people, and that makes it special."

I've heard *that* a million times. Grandpa has a story to tell about every single coin. I think I've heard all of them about a million times, too.

"Look, sweet pea!" Grandpa snaps open a small plastic case and holds up a coin that's not silver and not gold. I lean closer. This is one I haven't seen before.

"This is a bronze two-cent piece from way back in 1864," he says.

"Wow! That's a million years ago!" Danny shouts.

"Closer to a hundred fifty," I say, doing the math quickly in my head.

"Yes," Grandpa nods. "My father had an uncle, Charley Long, who fought in the Civil War. Uncle Charley saved this coin and passed it down to my father, who passed it down to me. Someday I'll pass it on to you." Grandpa is looking right at me. It's clear that this coin means a lot to him.

Grandpa sits back on the sofa and examines the two-cent piece. "This coin was part of your great-great-granduncle Charley's first pay after he became a soldier," Grandpa explains. "He sent his money home to his parents, and his mother kept this one coin all during the war—she carried it with her every day. It reminded her that one day the war would end, and she hoped with all her strength that her son, Charley, would come home safely."

Grandpa's story gives me goose bumps. There's nothing like a war keeping our family apart, but I can't help thinking that I miss my parents as much as great-great-granduncle Charley must have missed his.

"Then what happened?" Danny asks.

Grandpa smiles at Danny. "Well, Charley came

home from the war, safe and sound. His mother gave him this coin and told him how she'd kept it with her. So Charley decided to do the same thing. He carried this coin in his pocket every day until he passed it down to my father. He told my father to carry it as a reminder of his family."

I think of my own family. It's almost seven o'clock. Dad's going to Skype in soon, and I still don't know how I'm going to tell him about my test. I need a minute to think, so I go to my room and change into my polka-dot PJ's.

I pull my social studies test out of my backpack and set it on my desk. Danny's making some commotion out in the hallway, so I open my door to check it out. He's dragging part of Grandpa's coin collection into his room! "Hey!" I whisper. "Give me that, or you'll be in big trouble!"

"Like you?" he whispers back. I try to grab the box away from Danny, but he yanks it out of my reach. Then he drops it. Plastic sleeves and cases fall out. We both scramble to pick them up, hoping Grandpa hasn't heard us.

"I only wanted to get a closer look," Danny says.

"Dad's going to be on the computer in a few minutes," I tell Danny. "Go get your jammies on." Danny hops up and does a silly walk toward his room, imitating some ducks we saw at the zoo ages ago.

As awful as my day has been, Danny can still make me laugh. "And wash your face, Ducky!" I call after him. "You have mashed potato on your chin."

I take the box into my room. As I close the door, I hear Danny turn the water on in the bathroom. Down the hall, Gran asks Grandpa if he wants a cup of coffee. As I turn to set the box on my desk, I step on something. It's the plastic case holding the two-cent coin from great-great-granduncle Charley. It must have landed in my room when Danny dropped everything.

I pick it up, snap open the case, and examine the coin more closely. Grandpa usually polishes his coins, but this one has some dirt crusting over the date stamp. I use my thumbnail to rub the numbers 1864. My fingers start to tingle, and I feel dizzy. I close my eyes for a second and shiver from a gust of cold air. When I open my eyes, I can't quite believe what I see.

☺ *Turn to page 14.*

I'm still holding the coin, but I'm not in my room anymore. Instead, I'm outside, on a pier, standing next to an enormous ship. Somehow my PJ's have been replaced by a faded dress. I've also got on thin wool stockings, black lace-up boots, a scratchy shawl, and a bonnet with frayed ribbons tied under my chin. Another gust of wind sweeps over me, and I shiver again. It's cold, and whatever I'm wearing isn't nearly warm enough. Where did these clothes come from? Where am I?

Wherever I am, there are boats—and people— everywhere. The ships docked along the waterfront seem really old-fashioned—they're all made of wood and have giant sails. Workers scurry to steady huge crates that swing from ropes overhead as they're unloaded from the ships.

A steady stream of people starts leaving one of the ships. Most of the women are well dressed in long, full skirts and fancy bonnets, and the men wear suits with long coats and tall black hats. Some carry cloth bags, while others give directions to crew members struggling with large trunks. A few people from the boat walk onto the pier carrying nothing but small bundles. Their clothes look as worn as mine. These travelers are all African American, and they stand in a small group next to a stack of crates. Some are as old as my grandparents, and there are children in the group, too. They all seem unsure of what to do next.

I notice a horse-drawn wagon stopping at the end of the pier. I can't help staring. *Horses?* I look up and down the street, realizing that I don't see any cars. I don't see anything modern. Now I don't just wonder where I am—I wonder what year it is.

An older African American man in a suit climbs down from the front of the wagon, and several people hop off the back of the open bed. The man motions my way—is he waving at me? I duck behind the crates, not sure I want to talk to anyone.

Peeking around the crates, I see a girl about my age standing next to the man from the wagon. She's wearing a blue dress, worn boots, and a faded shawl, but her smile is bright and friendly. The group from the ship starts to move toward the wagon. Suddenly the people from the ship and the people from the wagon are shaking hands and hugging one another as though they're long-lost friends.

I'm so confused. Where am I? What's going on? The only thing that looks familiar is Grandpa's coin, which I'm still holding. I remember rubbing it, like this. My thumbnail scratches across the raised date on the two-cent piece. Instantly I feel dizzy again, and another gust of cold air makes me shiver.

I blink, and I'm back in my bedroom, wearing my polka-dot PJ's. I'm still holding the coin. How can this be happening? Grandpa's coin box is on my desk, right next to my social studies test. I hear water running in the bathroom, and Gran asking Grandpa if he wants a cup of coffee. Everything is the same as I left it. In fact, it seems to be the same moment I left. I was definitely somewhere else, but while I was gone, no time passed here at home!

"Wow!" I almost shout, before I clap my hand over my mouth. I look at the two-cent piece. Grandpa was right. It really *is* something special. Whatever just happened to me happened because of this coin. But how? I sink down on my bed, puzzled but amazed.

I wonder if I can go back in time again. I'm curious about the people on the pier and the girl by the wagon. I don't have any idea where I was, but finding out would sure be more fun than being grounded—or telling Dad I failed a test. No one at home will even know that I'm gone. I bite my lip, thinking. *Why not?* I decide. *I can always come home.*

Ready for another trip back in time, I squeeze the coin in my hand. Nothing happens. But then I hold the coin on my palm and scratch my thumb across the numbers 1864. My fingers start to tingle again, and I feel the now-familiar shiver. I'm not afraid. I'm excited!

☺ ***Turn to page 18.***

In an instant I'm back on the pier, behind the crates, wearing the same dress and shawl I had on the last time. Before I do anything, I make sure I have the coin. It's my way home, so I can't lose it. I tear a piece of fabric from the edge of my frayed shawl and use it to wrap the coin, knotting the cloth securely. Then I tuck the coin into the pocket of my dress.

I peer around the crates, and the girl with the smile is still there by the wagon. Good! I step out from my hiding spot and start to navigate my way through the crowd. I'm almost at the wagon when I bump into a man wearing one of those tall black hats. He glares at me as if I've just insulted him.

"Watch where you're going, colored girl!" he yells. The tone of his voice makes me jump. He's really angry with me. "You people should remember to keep your place!" he adds before rushing away.

My heart is racing. Jeepers. It was just an accident! I don't understand why he had to be so fierce. Why did he call me "colored"? Isn't that a not-very-nice word for black people? And what did he mean by "keep my place"? Don't I have just as much right to be here as anyone else?

I look around to see if anyone saw what happened, but no one stops or even seems to notice me. Will everyone be as rude as that man was? I feel the coin in my pocket and remind myself that I can go home whenever I want.

Through the crowd, I see the girl. She's wrapping a blanket around the shoulders of a thin woman who is sitting in the back of the wagon. When she turns, the girl catches my eye and smiles. "Hello," she shouts over the hustle and bustle around us. "Welcome to Philadelphia!"

☺ *Turn to page 20.*

P hiladelphia? So that's where I am. Isn't it known as the City of Brotherly Love? Someone forgot to explain that to the man in the tall hat.

I approach the wagon. "My name's Addy Walker," the girl says. "Welcome to freedom!"

"Freedom?" I repeat. I'm confused.

"Yes!" Addy says, taking both my hands. "You're not a slave no more!"

But I never was a slave, I say to myself. I think of Grandpa's coins and his Civil War stories. When the Civil War was over, slavery was over too. Grandpa told us that lots of people escaped that horrible life before the war ended, though. Did great-great-grand-uncle Charley's coin transport me to Philadelphia during the Civil War?

"You're safe now," Addy says. "We're from the Freedom Society at my church, Trinity A.M.E. We come to the pier to meet people new to freedom. We're gonna help you settle in."

"Thank you," I say, still feeling confused.

"Who you with?" Addy asks, looking around.

Another gust of wind sweeps past, and my teeth chatter for a moment. "N-No one," I answer truthfully,

wrapping my shawl more tightly around my shoulders. "I'm alone."

Addy's eyes grow wide. "You *all* alone? My family is separated, too, but I came here with my momma. At least we've got each other. I still miss Poppa and Sam and Esther every single day. That kind of missing is like a toothache that never goes away."

Now my eyes are wide. I'm shocked to hear that Addy's been separated from her family. But I hear something in her voice that makes me feel less alone: understanding. Addy knows what it's like to miss her dad. None of my friends get it, but Addy does. I wonder who Sam and Esther are. Suddenly I want to know everything about Addy.

Before I can ask any questions, Addy points to the man in the suit. "That's Reverend Drake," Addy says. He helps a few of the older people climb into the back of the wagon, and then he takes his place in the front and picks up the reins. "We're going back to the church now. Come on," Addy says.

The two of us follow behind the wagon, walking with the rest of the people from the pier. I stick close to Addy because the narrow sidewalk is full of people

and I don't want to get lost. Philadelphia is much bigger than my hometown, and I suddenly feel very small. It doesn't help that all the women are wearing long, full dresses. The uneven cobblestone sidewalk is barely wide enough for two women walking next to each other, and it's impossible for anyone to get past their skirts and walk around them. How would it feel to wear something so big and swishy? How does anyone sit down wearing a dress like that? I suddenly want to put on one of those skirts and try.

When we get to the corner, we stop at the edge of a broad street that's crowded with traffic. I've never seen so many horses! They're pulling wagons and carts, and the steady flow makes it impossible for us to cross. While we wait, I look at the shops that stretch down the street. There's one selling baskets and brooms, a fish market, a gun repair store, a butcher shop, and something that might be a women's clothing store. There are gloves and shawls in the window, but I'm baffled by the bell-shaped cages that are hanging outside the shop, above the front door. They look as if they're made of wire. What are they? I'd like to take a closer look—the shop's only halfway down the block—but Addy's pointing in the other direction where a crowd is forming one street over.

"It's soldiers," Addy says. "Soldiers marching off to war. Should we go see? We can catch up to Reverend Drake in a minute."

> ☉ *To watch the soldiers,*
> *turn to page 26.*

> ☉ *To explore the shop window,*
> *turn to page 28.*

Addy, my family's not coming to Philadelphia. I'm going to them," I explain. "I don't need to talk to Mr. Cooper. I just need to keep going."

"You've got to get to your family," Addy agrees. I can tell she's disappointed, even though she understands. "I just thought you was gonna be with us for a little while," she says. "Having you here has been like having a sister again."

"You and your mother have treated me like family. Thank you so much for everything you've done!"

"Will you be okay?" Addy asks.

"Yes, I promise. Now you get home. Your mother's going to be worried about you."

Addy hugs me. "You're so brave," she whispers. "I won't forget you."

You're the brave one, Addy, I think as I watch her hurry down the cobblestone sidewalk. *You don't know when you're going to see your family again, but you have hope. You worked so hard for your freedom, and even though you still can't do certain things because of the color of your skin, you don't get discouraged. You've been in school such a short time, but you're one of the smartest girls I've ever met.*

Addy stops at the corner and turns to wave at me

one last time. I wave back. *I won't ever forget you either, Addy Walker.*

I reach for the coin in my pocket. Addy has shown me how to make the best of what happens. I'm going to work hard in school and study all my subjects—not just the ones I like. I'm going to tell Dad about my failed test, and I can promise that it won't happen again, because I won't let it. And instead of counting the hours we're apart, I'm going to enjoy every minute I spend with my family when we're together. Plus, I have some riddles to tell Danny.

☺ *The End* ☺

To read this story another way and see how different choices lead to a different ending, turn to page 35.

I think of Grandpa. He'd be thrilled to see real Civil War soldiers. I nod and follow Addy, and we find a spot along the street.

I've seen parades before on the Fourth of July, but this is very different. There isn't a big band, and no one's throwing candy. There's one drummer leading the group, and he's playing a solemn beat that seems to echo in my chest. The soldiers march past in perfect lines. They stand straight and tall in their blue uniforms with shiny brass buttons. Their faces are serious and proud.

Many people around us cheer and applaud, but I notice that not everyone is happy. Some women and children are crying. I realize that these soldiers could be their sons and brothers—or even fathers. They're not marching for fun. They're marching off to war.

I feel the coin in my pocket and think of great-great-granduncle Charley. When I got up this morning, I didn't even know that I had a relative who fought in the Civil War. Now I feel almost as if I'm watching my own family member march off to battle with the rest of these men. Is this what Grandpa meant when he said that history is about real people?

"My brother, Sam, wanted to be a soldier," Addy says. Her voice wavers a bit, and she takes a breath before continuing. "He wanted to fight for freedom. Maybe he's doing that right now."

Before I can ask Addy anything about her brother, she asks me if I have any siblings.

"I have a younger brother," I answer, thinking of Danny's silly duck walk. All of a sudden, I miss him.

Addy must see that in my face, because she puts her arm around my shoulder. "You've had a long journey," she says. "Let's get to the church."

☺ *Turn to page 36.*

Actually," I say, "there's something over here I'd like to look at. Something I've never seen before." I nod toward the shop and take a tentative step that way.

"Freedom full of things you've never seen before," Addy says, her eyes bright. "What is it?"

The two of us make our way to the store, and I point at the big bell-shaped cages above the door. "What *are* those?" I ask.

"Hoops for hoopskirts!" Addy says.

The word is so funny that I start giggling. "HOOP-skirts," I repeat, drawing out the O's. "You sound like an owl."

That makes Addy giggle. "That sounds like something my brother, Sam, would say," she says with a wide smile. "Hoops is what makes ladies' dresses so wide," Addy explains. "My momma's a seamstress, and she says she has to use yards and yards of fabric to make a skirt wide enough to fit over a hoop like that. That's why a dress cost so much money."

I'm amazed. Women *wear* those contraptions? "Does your mother have a hoopskirt?" I ask.

Addy shakes her head. "Not one that big. Those are

just for rich ladies who dress up real fancy."

A woman comes out of the shop carrying a package, and suddenly I have an idea. "Addy, let's go in. Let's try on a hoopskirt!"

Addy looks at me as if I've suggested we go jump in the river. "We can't do that!" she says.

I think of going shopping with my mom and the way she always talks to the salespeople. "Oh," I say. "Do you have to have your mother with you?"

Addy shakes her head. "This is a store for white ladies," Addy says. "They don't let colored folks shop here."

I'm about to ask Addy if there's a store where we can shop, but she takes my elbow and steers me back toward the corner. "Come on," she says. "Let's go to the church."

☺ *Turn to page 36.*

ow it's *your* bedtime, girls," Mrs. Walker says when she and Addy stop singing.

As Addy and I undress, I notice her cowrie-shell necklace again. I think of how it connects her to family—even the people she never knew. I touch the coin in my pocket and start to wonder about my distant relatives. What were Charley's parents like? What did he do after the war? Suddenly I want to hear all of Grandpa's stories, and this time, really listen. He's always saying that history is about people. Now I get it.

Addy falls asleep quickly, but I lie awake. After an hour or so, Mrs. Walker blows out the candle and crawls into bed, too. I still can't sleep. It's time for me to go home.

Quietly, I get out of bed, dress quickly, and reach into Addy's school bag. By the light of the moon, I write a note on Addy's slate.

> *I have gone to find my family. Don't worry. I will be okay. You and your mother helped me have hope. I won't ever forget you.*

I tiptoe out of the garret and into the stairwell,

closing the door softly behind me. I take the coin out of my pocket. "Yoo-hoo, moon," I whisper. "I'll be home soon!"

☺ *The End* ☺

To read this story another way and see how different choices lead to a different ending, turn to page 94.

ddy walks to the end of the block and then turns to wave a last good-bye. I wave back. Once she's out of sight, I step into a nearby alley, looking to make sure no one else is around. Then I pull out great-great-granduncle Charley's coin. I look at the date. 1864. The year I learned what the word "family" really means. As soon as I rub the numbers between my fingers, I start to get dizzy and close my eyes.

When I open my eyes, I'm back in my bedroom, wearing my polka-dot PJ's. I blink a few times because the electric lights seem so bright after the lamps and candles of 1864. The heat steadily flowing out of the vents warms me to my toes, and I feel incredibly lucky to be so comfortable. I'm home!

I throw open my door and rush across to the bathroom, where Danny is running water to float his toy dinosaur in the sink. "Hurry up, Ducky!" I shout, rubbing his head. He shuts the tap off and frowns at me. "Let's go!" I grab his wet hand and pull him along toward the living room.

Gran and Grandpa are sitting on the sofa in front of the laptop. "What's all the ruckus?" Gran asks.

Just then we hear the sound of the car pulling into

the driveway. Mom comes bustling in with her books and bags.

"Mom!" I say, throwing my arms around her before she can put her stuff down. "You're home early!"

Mom drops everything to give me a squeeze. "I just decided that I needed some family time tonight," she says. "Did I miss Dad's call?"

Grandpa shakes his head. "Matter of fact, he e-mailed that he might be later than usual this evening," he says.

Mom plops down on the sofa and kicks off her shoes. Danny climbs into her lap, and I manage to snuggle between her and Gran. I'm surrounded by people I love. I feel Dad's presence among us even though he's miles away.

"So what are you all up to?" Mom asks.

"We're just spending some time together," I say, looking around at everyone. "Nothing special." But I know that being together is very special. In fact, it's awesome.

☺ *The End* ☺

To read this story another way and see how different choices lead to a different ending, turn to page 94.

n our way home, we pass a small building with a small painted sign that reads *Children's Theater.*

"Oh, Addy, let's go in!" I open the door and crane my neck to see inside. "It's a puppet show. Let's watch!"

"I don't know," Addy says slowly. "That show may not be for girls like us."

I drag her inside where I see a flyer on the wall. "This says the show is free for children."

"Well, all right," Addy says. "Maybe we can take a quick look." But she sounds hesitant.

We walk into the darkened theater toward a small stage. There's a large crowd of children and adults seated around the raised platform, and someone is playing a banjo to go along with the performance.

"Can you see anything?" Addy asks me.

"No." We stand on tiptoe, trying to see the stage. Then Addy finds us a spot with a better view. We're just about to sit down when a woman in an ugly hat taps me on the shoulder.

"You don't belong here," she says in a low voice.

"But the show is free," I tell her. "I read the flyer."

Addy leans to whisper in my ear. "She means

colored people ain't allowed!"

There's that term "colored" again. It must be okay to say it in Addy's time. "Why not?" I whisper back.

Addy only shrugs. "We just ain't."

"You need to leave before there's trouble," the woman says.

As the two of us head toward the door, I can feel the woman's eyes watching us. But when a couple of kids run past us, the woman marches off after them. "Hold on, Addy. She's not looking. Let's go around to the other side."

"Maybe we should just leave," Addy says. "We could go to Sarah's house. If she's done helping her momma, we could all do Double Dutch together."

It would be fun to jump rope again. But there wasn't anything on the flyer that said we couldn't watch the puppet show. The woman may not even be in charge.

⊙ *To watch from another part of the theater, turn to page 154.*

⊙ *To leave and go see Sarah, turn to page 160.*

here you from?" Addy asks me as we hurry to catch up to Reverend Drake's wagon.

"Tennessee," I say.

"That's a long way from Pennsylvania—especially all by yourself," Addy says. "Momma and I escaped from a plantation in North Carolina."

"You escaped?" I ask in awe.

Addy nods. "Momma and Poppa were planning for all of us to run away together. They were keeping it secret, but I heard them whispering about it one night when they thought I was asleep. Poppa had a plan to make it to Philadelphia. Momma wanted to wait for the war to be over, but Poppa said we couldn't wait no more. We had to take our freedom."

That sounds dangerous. "Oh, Addy, weren't you scared?" I ask.

"I was real scared. Sam ran off once. Master Stevens tracked him down . . ."

Addy stops talking for a moment. Her face clouds over, and I can tell that what she's thinking about isn't a good memory.

"Master Stevens tracked him down with dogs," Addy continues. "He brought Sam back to the

plantation and tied him to a tree and gave him a whipping."

I don't know what to say. All I can do is take Addy's hand and hold it until she's ready to talk again.

"After that," Addy continues, "any time Sam talked about running away again, my parents would tell him to hush up. But this time was different. We were going to go as a family and stay together."

But Addy's family isn't together. "What happened?" I ask as we stop at another busy corner.

Addy waits for the traffic to clear before leading me across the street. "Master Stevens sold Poppa and Sam," she says quietly.

"What?" I hear myself almost shouting. *How could a person sell someone else?*

"Momma said we were still going to run," Addy says when we reach the sidewalk. "I thought we were gonna wait for the war to end and for Poppa and Sam to come back for us, but Momma said they weren't ever coming back to the plantation. The day after I heard Poppa and Momma whispering, Poppa told Sam about the plan to go to Philadelphia. So someday, Poppa and Sam are gonna meet us here.

"I hope it's someday soon," I tell her. "The war can't last forever."

"That's just what Momma says, too. She says we gotta have hope. And patience."

"Your mother sounds a lot like my grandmother!" I say. "My dad left before I . . . um . . . came to Philadelphia. Whenever I miss him, Gran reminds me to keep hope in my heart."

"You're right. They do sound the same!" Addy smiles. "That's why I like to come to the pier. I keep hoping that someday I'm gonna see Sam or Poppa come off one of those ships."

"That's going to be a good day," I tell Addy. I think of waiting for the day my dad gets to come home. I know when that day is. It's circled in red on the calendar in my bedroom. Until then, I can e-mail him whenever I want, and we can talk every night. How does Addy go to sleep not even knowing where her dad and brother are? That's when I remember Addy talking about someone named Esther.

When I ask who Esther is, the smile leaves Addy's face. "Esther's my baby sister. We had to leave her behind with my Auntie Lula and Uncle Solomon.

Momma said they were too old to run, and Esther was too little. We couldn't carry a baby all the way to Philadelphia, and her crying would have made it impossible to hide. Now we here, but they ain't."

"That's awful," I say, thinking about Danny and my grandparents. What if they were gone and I didn't know when I'd see them again? I wonder how old great-great-granduncle Charley was when he went off to war. How long was he separated from his family?

Reverend Drake stops the wagon in front of a tall redbrick building. Addy stops, too. "We're at the church now," she says. "I been talking on and on about my family, and I ain't even asked about yours. Come inside and tell me about them."

I let Addy lead me through the wide-open doors. Just inside the door of the church, flyers are posted on the wall. There's one for a benefit for the Freedom Society. It's happening in November. November 1864. I touch the coin in my pocket. That's the year on great-great-granduncle Charley's two-cent piece!

☺ *Turn to page 43.*

S ixth Street School isn't far from Trinity A.M.E. Church. When we get to Addy's classroom, a few things look familiar. The desks are in rows, and groups of kids are gathered together, talking and laughing before class starts. Other things are very different. There's a black stove in the corner, like the one in Addy's room, but bigger. It's lit, and the room is warm. There are chalkboards on the wall instead of whiteboards. There aren't any computers or TVs.

All the kids look about my age, and some of them are dressed as I am in faded clothes and worn shoes. Others are wearing fancy dresses or crisply ironed shirts with funny bow ties. Everyone is African American. There isn't a single white person in the class. No one is Asian or Hispanic.

Addy shows me where to hang my shawl and bonnet. She calls it a cloakroom. Two other girls come in just as we're leaving.

"Hi, Sarah!" Addy says happily. "Hello, Harriet," she adds.

"Morning, Addy!" a round-faced girl with short hair answers. She hangs her thin, patched jacket next to Addy's shawl, and then she gives me a big smile.

The other girl takes off a fancy coat. She's wearing a beautiful yellow dress that's decorated with white lace. She looks ready for a party rather than a day at school. She doesn't say anything as she stares at my wrinkled dress.

"Hello," I say after Addy introduces us. But the girl named Harriet has already turned away. She's taking a small hand mirror from her pocket to check her shiny black curls. I look at Addy and Sarah, who shrug and head back to the classroom.

There are girls who aren't very friendly in my school. I guess there are snooty girls in 1864, too.

Addy takes me to meet the teacher. I'm a little nervous, but Miss Dunn puts me at ease right away.

"Welcome!" she says, shaking my hand. "I know adjusting to freedom isn't easy. I didn't go to school myself until my family escaped slavery."

"You were a slave?" I blurt out.

"Yes, I was," Miss Dunn says. "I remember my first few days of school. I felt confused at first, but things got easier. I'm sure Addy will help you."

"I sure will," Addy agrees.

When Miss Dunn goes to her desk and rings a

small handbell, everyone scurries to their seats. Addy shows me to a double desk near the middle of the room. Sarah sits in the row beside us, and Harriet is at the desk in front of us.

Addy leans close to me. "Do you know your letters?" she asks. I nod, confused by her question. Doesn't everyone our age?

☺ *Turn to page 92.*

Addy takes me to the basement of the church and into a large meeting hall. I have to squint to see in the dim light. *Of course*, I think. *No electricity in 1864.* The room is lit by candles hanging from fixtures on the wall.

The room is full of people, and I get hugged over and over again. When Addy tells everyone that I'm on my own, I get hugged even more. They all make me feel very welcome!

There are long tables piled with food, and my stomach begins to make noises. I think of Grandpa's bluefish and realize that I didn't eat much dinner. I'm hungry.

After Addy and I take off our shawls and bonnets, I follow her to a table where a woman is dishing out servings of a thick pudding. "Momma," Addy says, "I want you to meet my new friend."

"Hello," Addy's mother says, smiling at me. "I'm Mrs. Walker. You must be tired and hungry." She turns to Addy. "Sit your friend down. You and me gonna get her a plate of food and some of my sweet-potato pudding."

Addy insists that I rest while she and her mother

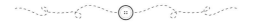

get me something to eat. I sit and wait, watching the others in the room. I recognize the ones from the pier. They're eating as if they haven't had food in days. Even in the dim light, I realize how worn-out and dirty and sad some of them look. What were their journeys to freedom like? I can only imagine what they've been through.

Addy and her mother come back with two plates full of chicken, cornbread, some kind of greens, and a helping of sweet-potato pudding. There's a pitcher of water on the table, and Mrs. Walker pours two cups. "You two eat," she says. "I gonna help with the serving. Addy, keep taking good care of your new friend."

"What is *your* family like?" Addy says, taking a bite of cornbread.

"There's my mother and father and my little brother, Danny," I explain. "And my grandparents. They help take care of us because . . . because my parents can't right now." I look down at my plate before I add, "I really miss my parents, especially my father."

Addy nods, as if she knows exactly how I feel.

As we talk, I realize that Addy *does* know how I feel. She misses her family the same way I miss mine.

But the more Addy describes her life in Philadelphia, the more I realize that her family's separation is much, much more serious than mine.

"Addy," I ask. "How did you and your mother escape?"

Addy puts her fork down. "Auntie Lula and Uncle Solomon got us disguises," she begins. "That way, Master Stevens's dogs couldn't track our scents. We left in the middle of the night, and we ran as fast as we could while it was dark. If there was water, we ran through it to throw off the dogs. We crossed one river that was real swift, and Momma . . ." Addy shivers. "Momma almost drowned."

"Oh, no!" I whisper.

Addy only nods. "Momma can't swim. Her foot got caught on some branches along the bottom of the river. I had to swim underwater and get her loose. The moon was full that night, but it was dark in the water. I was real scared."

Addy's quiet for a long moment before she goes on. "After we got out of the water, it was hard to see where we were going. But we kept going. When it started to get light, we had to hide. One morning we found a cave, and another day we slept under a tree, with some branches covering over us. Momma had a little bit of food for us, and some water, but all I could think about was finding the safe house."

"The safe house," I repeat. I remember learning about those in school. I never imagined I would meet someone who had to use one.

Addy nods. "A woman named Miss Caroline let us in. She fed us and gave us different clothes." Addy indicates the blue dress she's wearing. "Then she hid us in her wagon and took us to the coast where we got on the ship that brought us to Philadelphia. And that's how we got here."

The sweet-potato pudding is a lump in my throat. "Addy, you truly are the bravest person I've ever met."

Addy smiles at me. "You're brave, too. You're by yourself. Or you were. Now you have the church to help. And you have a friend. Me!"

⊙ *Turn to page 48.*

ddy freezes, and so do I. The man looks down his nose at us. "You look like two of the runaway slaves I'm searching for. Let me see your papers!"

"What papers?" I whisper to Addy.

"Freedom papers," she whispers back. "This ain't good!"

"But we're not slaves!" I tell the man.

"I can explain," Addy adds.

I've got a bad feeling about this. I think we should run, but Addy knows a lot more about surviving in 1864. Should I let her do the talking?

☺ *To run away,*
   turn to page 51.

☺ *To let Addy try to explain,*
   turn to page 52.

I'm glad you're my friend, Addy," I say sincerely. "If I hadn't met you, I don't think I would have stayed in Philadelphia for long."

"Well, you could have gone to the Quaker Aid Society here in Philadelphia," Addy tells me as we take our empty plates to a table at the back of the hall. "They help people, 'specially folks looking to meet up with their families. Momma says the Quaker Aid Society's good at helping people keep their hope alive.

"I think you'll like Philadelphia," Addy goes on. "It takes some time to get used to it since it's so big and loud. But we can go to school! You'll come with me tomorrow, won't you?" Addy's face is so happy, it's as if she's talking about going to a water park instead of school.

"I guess so," I say reluctantly, thinking about my failed grade. I'm pretty sure I won't ever be as excited about school as Addy is.

"You can sit with me," she continues happily. "We've got double desks, and you can be my desk partner! Miss Dunn, our teacher, is real nice." Addy looks at me, and her face suddenly becomes serious. "It's okay if you can't read or write," she assures me.

"Not knowing something is nothing to be 'shamed about. Miss Dunn will help you, and so will I."

Addy's mother is at the table in back where we return our plates. "Momma," Addy says, "can my new friend stay with us? She's separated from her family."

"You all by yourself?" Mrs. Walker asks. "Of course you can stay with us!"

"Thank you," I say. I hadn't even thought about where I would stay—or even how long I would stay.

"You girls can go on home now. I need to talk to Reverend Drake about the benefit for the Freedom Society."

I wonder if I've heard right. Addy's mother just gave us permission to go somewhere alone?

"I won't be long after you. Be real careful!" she warns. Now she sounds more like my mom.

"It's only a short walk," Addy says as we put on our bonnets and shawls. "We live above the dress shop where Momma works."

When we get outside, the sun is still shining brightly. "My momma makes the most beautiful dresses!" Addy tells me as we head down a busy street.

"My mom tried to teach me to sew. She says I'm

hopeless with a needle and thread," I say. Addy and
I laugh together. We're out of sight of the church when
a plump red-haired man steps out of nowhere, blocking
our way.

"You, there!" he shouts at us. "Stop!"

⊙ *Turn to page 47.*

I grab Addy's hand and start running. I don't know where I'm going. I just want to get away from the man who thinks we're slaves.

"This way!" Addy says, pulling me down an alley. I see what looks like a dead end ahead, but Addy keeps going toward a wooden fence that's twice as tall as we are. I look over my shoulder, and the red-haired man is barreling behind us, breathing hard.

I turn back just in time to see Addy disappear into the fence. *How in the world did she do that?* I wonder— right before I trip on a loose cobblestone and fall.

Addy's on the other side of the fence, pushing aside a plank to let me through. I can see that the space is just big enough for me to squeeze past. "Hurry!" Addy cries.

I scramble to my feet and dive for the opening in the fence, tugging on my skirt to pull it through in time. But someone is pulling it from the other side.

"Addy, he's got my skirt!"

☺ *Turn to page 54.*

you're making a mistake," Addy pleads. "We're free! My momma works for—" But the man cuts her off.

"You keep quiet!" he growls, searching in his vest pocket. "I know I've got an advertisement here somewhere for the likes of you."

He pulls out a pack of newspaper clippings and begins to flip through them. "Lemme see. Georgia, Mississippi . . ." He looks from the papers to us and then back to the papers again. "Alabama . . ."

I decide to speak up. I try to keep my voice calm, the way Gran is always reminding me to do when I've got something important to say. "Sir? We are not who you think we are. We—"

Before I can finish, the man cuts me off, too. "I said quiet!" His eyes are blazing with anger. "You darkies don't know anything. These here slave owners—" He shakes the papers at us, "are looking for their runaway property!"

I shudder at the idea that someone could think of Addy and me as property instead of people. But this man clearly does. Why?

"I get paid right nicely for bringing said property

back where it belongs," the man finishes.

It's the money, I realize. These people look at slaves as a way to make money.

The thought reminds me of the money I have in my pocket—great-great-granduncle Charley's two-cent piece. I could rub it right now and get out of all of this. But what about Addy? She looks as terrified as I feel. I think about her and her mother escaping the plantation and risking their lives to make it to freedom. I can't let this man take Addy back to slavery. I won't leave her.

I scan the crowd on the sidewalk. Will someone help us? That's when I see a man in a uniform. "Addy," I whisper. "Is that a police officer?"

Addy nods, and her eyes go from scared to hopeful. We both start waving our arms and yelling.

☉ *Turn to page 56.*

 won't let him get *you*!" Addy says, grabbing both my hands. I can hear the edge of my skirt ripping as Addy pulls me free. We're in another alley, and my heart is pounding.

Addy helps me stand up. "Catch your breath," she tells me. "He too big to squeeze through the fence after us, so he'll have to come 'round the corner. We gonna cut through this alley and circle back to the church."

I reach into my pocket. Is the coin still there? It is! I could use it right now and go home. But what about Addy? I can't leave her. "Who is that man?" I ask, leaving the coin in my pocket.

"He's a slave catcher—a very bad man."

"But we're not slaves!" I protest.

Addy looks at me the same way I sometimes look at my little brother when he doesn't understand something obvious. "We're colored, and slavery's still goin' on in the South. If we ain't got special papers that say we're free, he can take us and sell us."

Before I can ask any more questions, I hear a noise at the end of the alley. Is it the slave catcher?

☺ *Turn to page 58.*

on't listen to her, Addy!" Sarah says, stepping between Addy and Harriet.

I shake my head at Harriet. "Come on, Addy," I say. "Let's go."

Sarah and I take Addy's hands. "You gonna see Esther again, Addy!" Sarah says. "I know you are."

"Sarah's right," I say. "Your whole family's going to be together again someday." In my heart, I hope that's true. Will Addy's family all be together once the war ends? I touch the coin in my pocket, knowing that I can see my own family whenever I want to. I wish I could use this mysterious power to do the same for my new friend.

"And anyway, Addy," I say loud enough for Harriet to hear, "I'd be honored to be your sister!"

Addy gives my hand a thank-you squeeze and then hugs each of us. "You two are the best friends I could have," she says.

☺ *Turn to page 123.*

fficer!" I yell.

"Help us!" Addy screams.

"Quiet!" the slave catcher roars, shoving the papers back into his pockets.

"What's all this?" the policeman asks, when he makes his way over to us.

"This man is trying to take us away!" I say.

"They're runaways," the slave catcher sighs.

"That's not true!" Addy says.

"Do you have papers?" the policeman asks, looking at me and Addy. We shake our heads.

He looks at the slave catcher. "You have papers on them?"

The redheaded man nods. "Back at the office."

The police officer pauses. "Very well, then. Move it along."

"No!" Addy shouts as the slave catcher takes her arm with one hand and mine with the other.

Wait. I can't believe what just happened. Is the police officer really going to let this awful man just drag us away? Doesn't anybody understand that this is not okay?

"Please, talk to Reverend Drake at Trinity A.M.E.

Church," Addy cries out to the police officer as the slave catcher pulls us toward the street. "He knows us! Please!"

The policeman only squints and watches as Addy and I are pulled to a small horse-drawn cart. Some people stare, but others act as if they can't see us at all.

⊙ *Turn to page 61.*

Addy tries to pull me into the shadows, but there's nowhere to hide. We hear scratching, then panting. Something moves. A yellow tail appears.

"It's only a dog," I say with relief. It's wagging its tail the same way Nikki's friendly mutt, Nemo, does when he meets me at her front door. I start to move toward the dog. But Addy holds me back.

"No," she says. "That dog might be dangerous."

Addy seems frozen to her spot. That's when I remember what she told me about Master Stevens's dogs. She's probably terrified of any dog. I would be too if I thought dogs were used to chase down people.

"I have a feeling this dog isn't going to hurt us," I say. "It's wagging its tail."

"Ain't you scared?" Addy asks, looking anxiously at the skinny, scruffy creature in front of us.

I think of the man chasing us. "Not of a dog," I answer. The dog walks toward us, sniffing the garbage in the alley, and then stops, blocking our way out of the alley. I pull Addy's arm. She's trembling.

"We have to go around him," I say.

Addy doesn't move. "Maybe it's a wild dog. Dog bites can be real bad."

I realize that I have to convince Addy that this dog
is safe. And I have to do it fast. The slave catcher will be
here any second.

"I don't think this dog will bite us," I tell Addy.
I take a few slow steps toward the dog and stop
several feet away from it. I hold my hand out, palm
down, the way Nikki taught me. "Hey, fella," I say
calmly. "Come and say hello."

Addy pulls in her breath. "Be careful!" she cries.

"It's okay," I say, as the dog approaches me. Its tail is
still wagging. It sniffs my hand and then licks it. After
a moment I slowly move my hand to the dog's ear and
scratch it. "See?" I say to Addy. "This dog wants to be
our friend."

Addy takes a cautious step toward me and the dog.

"We need to go," I tell her. " Can you do it?"

She nods and takes my hand, and together we run
past the dog to the open end of the alley. We peek
around the corner cautiously. I look one way, and Addy
looks the other. The street is crowded with horses and
wagons, but there are fewer people walking along this
narrow sidewalk.

"All clear!" I whisper.

"Uh-oh," Addy says.

I whip my head in the direction she's looking. It's the slave catcher!

☺ *Turn to page 63.*

et in!" the slave catcher barks, pointing to the back of the cart. Addy and I follow his order. We crouch together in the corner. Addy's face is blank, but I know she's scared. I understand now how serious this is. Really losing your freedom is nothing like being grounded.

"Where do you think he's taking us?" I whisper to Addy.

Her voice is shaky when she answers. "There's a place in town called the Slave Market. I ain't never been there."

I shudder and reach for Addy's hand. Addy squeezes it tightly. We bounce along the rough streets for a long time, and the city stretches on. I'm completely lost. The slave catcher finally stops the cart in front of a short brick building that sits between a bank and a store that sells men's hats. There's some fancy writing on the window. I gasp. It reads *Negroes for Sale*.

The slave catcher waves us out of the cart and into the building. Addy and I are still clutching each other's hands as we stumble through the door. "Stand over there," he says, pointing to a wall covered with flyers and advertisements.

We're in an office. There's a high counter across the front, with several desks behind it. It looks a little bit like the office where my mom works. I feel a sharp pang of homesickness when I think about Mom.

A man with white hair and glasses sits behind the counter. He frowns when the redheaded man goes to speak to him. Their voices drop, but they never take their eyes off us.

"Should we try to run again?" I whisper to Addy, even though I have no idea where we are or how to get back to the church.

Addy shakes her head. Her face is the same blank it was in the cart. For some reason, that makes me even more scared.

☺ *Turn to page 65.*

Let's get out of here!" I scream. I spring onto the sidewalk and start sprinting away from the red-haired man. Addy's right behind me.

I stop at the curb, not sure which way to go to get back to the church. When I look back over my shoulder, I catch a glimpse of the slave catcher.

Addy doesn't look back. She just grabs my hand and turns to the right. We don't stop running until we see the red brick of the church.

It takes us a few minutes to catch our breath. "I thought you were safe from people like that in Philadelphia," I finally say.

Addy shakes her head as we make our way down to the meeting hall. "I thought freedom would mean that I could go where I wanted, just like everybody else. But as long as there's still slavery, we've got to watch for slave catchers, even in the North," Addy says.

I don't know what to say. I can't tell Addy that the kind of freedom I wanted was to get ice cream without my mom waiting for me in the car. Now that seems so unimportant.

When we get to the meeting hall, we find Addy's mother talking to Reverend Drake.

"What are you two doing back here?" Mrs. Walker asks, looking from one of us to the other.

"We were chased by a slave catcher," Addy tells her.

Mrs. Walker looks horrified. "What? Some man was chasing you? Are you all right?"

"We're fine, Momma," Addy says. "But we had to run. It was like escaping from the plantation all over again." Addy's voice breaks, and her mother pulls her into a tight hug.

"What happened?" Reverend Drake asks.

After I tell him everything, he insists on walking us home.

Once we're on the sidewalk, Mrs. Walker holds firmly to both Addy's and my hands. I feel safer with her warm fingers wrapped around mine, but I'm still scared we'll see the red-haired man again.

⊙ *Turn to page 68.*

The man with the glasses stands up and starts walking toward us. But before he says or does anything, there's a commotion at the door. It bursts open, and the policeman from the street rushes in, along with Reverend Drake and Addy's mother.

"Momma!" Addy cries out, running to her.

Mrs. Walker wraps her arms around Addy. "You all right?" she asks.

I feel my eyes fill with tears. I'm so relieved, but I'm also suddenly desperate to see *my* mother. When Mrs. Walker motions to me, I cross the room and fling my arms around her waist. The three of us hold on to one another.

"You *do* know these girls?" the policeman asks Reverend Drake.

"I certainly do!" Reverend Drake says. "They're part of my congregation. I vouch for the freedom of these children, and I'd like to see any paper that says something different!" Reverend Drake looks directly at the redheaded man.

"Officer, I think my man here has made a mistake," the man with the glasses says.

"It appears so," the policeman replies, holding the

door open and motioning for Mrs. Walker, Addy, and me to leave. "You need to keep better records. Stop harassing the citizens of Philadelphia!"

Outside, the policeman turns to Addy. "You used your wits, young lady, when you told me about the Reverend. But be careful, both of you. This is a dangerous time for colored people."

"Yes, sir!" Addy and I say.

Reverend Drake helps us into the back of the same wagon that I first saw on the pier. Mrs. Walker sits in the front with the Reverend. On the way to the Walkers' home, I expect to get a Grandpa-type lecture about making good choices. Instead, Reverend Drake says, "Y'all were very lucky today."

"You were also brave," Mrs. Walker adds, looking at us over her shoulder. "I'm proud of you both. But I shouldn't have let you go by yourselves. That wasn't right."

"No, Ruth," the Reverend says quietly. "It's not right that these girls have to walk home in fear. It's proof that the fight for our freedom isn't happening only on the battlefields."

The Reverend's words give me chills. All the people

I met today who worked so hard to get to freedom still aren't free. Not truly. Not when they still have to prove they aren't someone else's property.

As we bump along the cobblestone streets, I realize that I'm shaking. What if Reverend Drake and Mrs. Walker hadn't gotten to us in time? Sure, I had the special coin in my pocket. But Addy . . . I don't even want to think of her back in slavery, maybe never seeing any of her family again. I squeeze her hand.

"I didn't know what to do today," I say weakly.

Addy puts a comforting arm around my shoulder. "Yes, you did," Addy reassures me. "You saw the police officer. You caught his ear with some good hollerin'." For the first time since we left the church, Addy smiles.

"You had quite a first day in freedom," she says, as the wagon comes to a stop in front of a narrow three-story building. "But we home now."

☺ *Turn to page 72.*

A t the dress shop, we thank Reverend Drake for walking us home. Then Addy and her mother lead me up two flights of steep stairs to the top floor.

I try to hide the surprise on my face when Mrs. Walker opens the door. Addy and her mother live in one room, and it's smaller than my bedroom at home. The wood floor is bare, and there are no curtains at the single window. The room is cold, and the only light is the late afternoon sun slanting through the window.

Mrs. Walker goes to the table in the middle of the room and lights a single candle. Addy takes off her shawl and bonnet and hangs them on a wooden peg on the wall. She turns to me, and I hand her my shawl and fumble with the ribbons under my chin. Addy hangs my things on the peg over hers.

"You two sit," Mrs. Walker says, taking off her own hat and wrap and putting on an apron. "You had quite a scare today. Momma's gonna make you something warm to drink."

Mrs. Walker goes to a squat black iron thing in the corner. It's connected to the wall by a thick pipe. When Mrs. Walker sets a saucepan on top of it, I realize that it's a stove. I look around the room as Addy and

I sit down at the table. There are only two chairs. There's also only one bed, and it's not very big. The only other furniture is a small table against the wall holding a white porcelain pitcher and a big white bowl. *This is everything they own*, I think.

Addy and her mother don't have much space, and they certainly don't have room for company, but Addy's clearly thrilled that I'm staying with them. Despite our frightening afternoon, she's watching me with a smile on her lips.

"Thank you again for letting me stay," I say.

Addy's face breaks into a full grin. "I've never had company before!" she says.

"We call it a sleepover," I tell her.

Addy giggles. "Momma, we're having a sleepover!"

Mrs. Walker has lit a fire in the stove, and the room is starting to feel warmer. She dips the saucepan into a bucket of water and then sets the pan back on the stove. "When you go to bed you're gonna pull that quilt over the top of you. Don't that make this a sleep*under*?" she asks.

Addy and I laugh. The light from the window is fading, and we sit in the glow of the candle. "Your

home is cozy," I tell her. Because suddenly, it is.

Addy looks across the room. "My favorite part is the window. Now I can see the sky. Back on the plantation, our cabin didn't have any windows. And we only had a dirt floor."

I don't know what to say. Addy has almost nothing, and yet she's excited about a window.

Mrs. Walker puts two cups on the table. Steam floats from the top, and I wrap my chilled fingers around the cup in front of me. I was expecting hot chocolate, which is what Gran always makes me and Danny. But maybe chocolate is a luxury for Addy and her mother.

"Mrs. Drake gave me a cinnamon stick today, so I shaved a little extra flavor in your tea. Drink it while it's hot."

"Mmmm. It good, Momma," Addy says.

I take a sip. It *is* good.

"Here's some sweet-potato pudding for our supper." Mrs. Walker puts a plate with a small serving on the table and sets two spoons next to it. There are no other chairs, so Addy's mother stands over us while we drink our tea and share the cold pie. Soon the warm tea and

the spices in the pie begin to relax me. I don't know what time it is—there's no clock in the room—but the sky outside the window is a deep purple. I yawn.

Mrs. Walker looks at me. "Both of you had a long day," she says. "As soon as you finish your tea, it's bedtime."

I don't argue. I'm tired. I look at the narrow bed in the corner. Are all three of us going to fit?

⊙ *Turn to page 75.*

The sign above the front window says *Ford's Dress Shop*. I'm still trembling as we climb out of the wagon. Seeing Addy's home makes me long for my own.

"Thank you so much, Reverend," Mrs. Walker says as she shakes the Reverend's hand. She cups Addy's cheeks in her hands and gives her a long look. "I don't know what I would do if something happened to my girl."

Mrs. Walker sounds just like my mother. Right now I want to see my mother so bad that I feel dizzy.

"Say thank you to the Reverend, girls," Mrs. Walker says.

"Thank you, Reverend Drake," Addy and I say at exactly the same time.

Reverend Drake tips his hat. "Our church family has got to look after one another, doesn't it?"

As the Reverend climbs back into his wagon, his words echo in my head. Family has to look after one another. I think of my family and how much my grandparents are helping while my parents work to make things better for Danny and me. I miss my grandparents. I miss everyone. I want to go home.

"Addy?" I say, just as Mrs. Walker is opening the door. Addy looks at me expectantly, and I feel bad about what I'm going to say. "I really appreciate everything you and your momma have done for me, but I can't stay."

Addy looks surprised. "But you have to!" she insists.

I shake my head. Mrs. Walker turns around. "What's this?" she asks.

"I need to keep traveling to meet my family," I say. I think about shopping with my mom and the way she always picks out a meeting place for us. "We have a meeting place, too, but it's not Philadelphia."

I can see that Addy is disappointed. "You got a long way to go?" she asks.

I feel great-great-granduncle Charley's coin in my pocket. "Not really," I answer.

Mrs. Walker folds her arms. "I know you've got a powerful need to see your family, but I want you safe, too. After today . . ."

I don't want Addy's mother to think I'm going to wander around the city by myself. But I can't tell her that a magic coin is going to send me into the future,

either. I remember Addy telling me that the Quaker
Aid Society helps people. I tell Mrs. Walker that that's
where I'm going.

"You sure about this?" Addy asks. I nod.

Mrs. Walker closes the door again. "Then Addy and
me gonna walk you over there," she says firmly.

⊙ *Turn to page 78.*

ddy and I undress for bed, and I make sure my coin is still in my pocket. When I take off my dress, I realize I'm wearing some kind of undershirt and long underpants that go past my knees.

Addy doesn't seem the least bit surprised by what I've got on. "You gonna sleep in your chemise?" she asks, putting on a long white nightgown.

"I guess so," I say, deciding to keep my stockings on for warmth. While Addy hangs her dress on the peg with our shawls and hats, I roll up my dress. The Walkers don't seem to have any pillows, so I'm going to use my dress.

I shiver as a chilly draft blows across the room from the window. There's only the last glow of a fire left in the stove. I quickly crawl under the quilt next to Addy, where we huddle together to keep warm.

"I used to sleep with my little sister, Esther, on a pallet," Addy says. "I was happy to see a real mattress when we moved here."

I don't know what a pallet is, but Addy's "real" mattress is so lumpy that I've already rolled over twice. I don't say anything about how uncomfortable this bed is—not when Addy's so proud of her home.

"I'm so tired I could sleep anywhere," I say, which is true, lumpy mattress or not.

In the flickering light of the candle, I see a dark leather string hanging around Addy's neck. "What's your necklace?" I ask.

Addy's eyes light up as she shows me a small white shell. "It a cowrie shell," she says proudly. "It belonged to my poppa's grandmother. She was stole from Africa when she was no bigger than us, and she came on a ship across the water all by herself. Momma says this was all she had from her home. She wore this shell on a necklace her whole life, and when she died, she gave it to my poppa's momma, who gave it to him. When we were running away, my momma gave it to me."

"It's beautiful," I tell Addy.

"The string is one of Sam's old shoelaces. That way, I've got something from him with me all the time, too," Addy says.

I touch the small shell, surprised by the strong connection Addy has to so many generations of her family. Addy's proud of her family's history. Maybe having real things like this, from long ago, is what makes history meaningful.

"Now, don't you worry about tomorrow," Addy says, yawning. "I'll be right by your side in school."

I smile in the near-dark. "Thank you, Addy."

"You're welcome," she says in a sleepy voice.

"Girls," Mrs. Walker says softly, "it's time to sleep now." She's at the table, bent over some cloth, sewing by the dim light of that single candle.

"'Night, Momma," Addy says, closing her eyes. "'Night," she whispers to me, squeezing my hand.

It's been an incredible day. I've learned about slavery in school, but hearing about it from Addy— and having to run away from it myself—is completely different.

My eyes begin to feel heavy. I'm totally exhausted. I give in to sleep, wondering what tomorrow will be like.

☺ *Turn to page 80.*

I t's a short walk to the Quaker Aid Society.
No one says much. Addy holds tight to her mother's hand and to mine. When we get to the building, I stop outside the door.

"I don't know how to thank you," I say to Addy and her mother.

Addy's mother smiles. "It's like the Reverend said: We've got to help one another."

"I'm glad I met you," Addy says. "I'm glad I got to be your friend."

"I'm glad, too. I'm glad I met *both* of you. I just wish things were easier for you."

"Nobody said freedom would be easy," Mrs. Walker replies. "There's a price to pay for what we really want, but that cost makes it real precious."

Somehow I know that what she's saying is true for me, too.

I squeeze Addy's hand. "Your family's always with you in your heart," I say. "I hope you're all together again really soon." We hug tightly.

Mrs. Walker touches my cheek. "Be safe, you hear?" she says softly.

"I will," I promise.

Addy and her mother leave me, but I don't move. Halfway down the block, Addy turns back and waves. I wave back, watching until they're out of sight. Then I duck into the alley next to the building, pull out my coin, and unwrap it from the piece of fabric. I take a deep breath and rub my thumb over the raised numbers. "Good-bye, 1864," I whisper. "Good-bye, Addy!"

☺ *Turn to page 86.*

When I open my eyes again, I'm not sure where I am. It must be early in the morning because there's a faint pink light coming from the window. Then I remember: I'm with Addy. I hear her steady breathing next to me.

I'm squeezed so tightly into the narrow bed with Addy and her mother that I can hardly move. I pop my arms out from under the quilt to stretch, but I pull them back in right away. The room that was chilly last night is downright cold this morning. The fire in the stove must have burned out long ago. I reach for the dress that I used as a pillow and find Grandpa's coin in the pocket, still wrapped in the piece of fabric. Good!

Addy stirs next to me. "You awake?" she whispers.

"I am!" I answer.

"We all are," Mrs. Walker says from the far side of the cramped bed. "We best get up and get the day started!"

"Come on, sleepy!" Addy laughs, throwing back the covers. She nudges me out of bed. When my stocking-covered feet hit the wooden floor, I shiver.

Addy notices. "Momma," she asks, "can't we light the stove? It's mighty cold!"

Mrs. Walker shakes her head as she buttons her dress. "No, Addy, honey. We only got enough coal to last through the week if we just use it to cook dinner." Her voice is gentle, but firm.

"Yes, Momma," Addy says.

I'm so cold that my fingers are numb. I'm tempted to crawl back under the covers, but Addy's already made the bed and is smoothing the quilt. How can the Walkers do without heat? Our house has never been cold during winter. I blink at their lonely-looking little black stove.

"You girls get dressed. That will warm you up. I'll fix you some breakfast," Mrs. Walker tells us.

I unfold the dress that I used as a pillow. It's pretty wrinkled. I didn't think about having to wear it again today. Maybe Addy could lend me one of her dresses. But when I see Addy putting on the same blue dress she wore yesterday, I realize she doesn't have any other clothes for herself, let alone me. My wrinkled dress will have to do.

"My hair must be a mess," I say. I look around for a mirror and realize there isn't one.

"Your hair's not too bad," Addy says. "Sit on the

bed. I'll fix it." In a few minutes, Addy has braided my hair into two braids and tied each with a black-and-white ribbon. They're the same checkered pattern as the ribbons in her hair.

"Momma got these from Mrs. Ford," she tells me. "They from the end of a roll."

"They're pretty," I say. "We're twins!"

"I guess we are!" Addy smiles. "Let's run down to the privy before we wash up for breakfast."

"Take the bucket and get some water," Mrs. Walker says, as we hurry out the door.

I wonder what a privy is, I think as I follow Addy.

We run down the steep staircase and outside, into the cold, dim alley beside the building. It smells awful, and there's garbage everywhere. In the middle of it all is a small wooden building about the size of a closet. There's a door with a little moon-shaped window cut into it. Is a privy an outdoor toilet?

The door is closed. "Somebody's in there," Addy explains. "Ten families share this privy. We can fill the bucket while we wait."

Addy shows me a pump on the side of the build-ing. She sets the bucket on the ground and grabs the

handle, moving the lever up and down several times. Nothing happens. Then a rush of water spits out. It looks kind of brown. Addy keeps pumping until the water's a bit clearer. Then she nudges the bucket with her foot until it's under the pump so that she can fill the bucket.

When she's done, the privy door opens and a boy a little older than us comes out. He and Addy nod to each other. "You go ahead and go first," Addy says.

I step into the privy and close the door. It smells horrible. It's worse than the port-o-potties we have to use when we go to the fair in the summer. I hold my breath and finish as quickly as I can.

Addy takes her turn, and we hurry back upstairs.

Now it feels warmer in the garret, even though the stove still isn't lit. Addy pours some of the water from the bucket into the porcelain pitcher on the small table against the wall. She stands over the big white bowl while I pour water from the pitcher into her cupped hands. She splashes the water onto her face, letting the water fall into the bowl. When she's done, she wipes her face and hands on a small towel hanging from the side of the washstand.

Then I do the same. My skin tingles when the cold water hits it. "Ohhh!" I gasp, grabbing for the towel.

"Hurry, now," Addy says. "We can't be late for school!"

"That's right," Mrs. Walker says. "Here's some cornbread for breakfast." She sets two bowls on the table.

The cornbread is good, but it's gone quickly and I'm still hungry. I think about Grandpa making stacks and stacks of banana pancakes and frying crisp bacon. At home, we eat until we're full, not until the food runs out.

While we eat, Mrs. Walker fills a tin pail that's got a scrap of green and white cloth tied to the handle. "There enough in this lunch pail for both of you," she says with a smile. Even though they don't have much, Addy and her mother are generous about sharing what they have with me.

"Thank you," I say.

"We all do what we can to help one another," Mrs. Walker tells me. Then she looks at Addy. "You go straight to school, now. And come straight home after. Be careful!"

"We will, Momma. I promise!" Addy says.

We put on our hats and shawls. Addy picks up her school bag, and I carry the lunch pail. "Let's go!" she says, pulling on my arm. I've never seen anyone so excited to go to school.

☺ *Turn to page 89.*

I'm standing in the middle of my room, wearing my polka-dot PJ's. I'm still holding great-great-granduncle Charley's coin, which feels warm in my hand. The first thing I do is put it back in its plastic case and tuck it safely into the box with the rest of Grandpa's coin collection. Then I throw open my bedroom door and listen. I hear Danny running water in the bathroom, and in the living room Gran is still asking Grandpa if he wants a cup of coffee. I'm home!

Hearing Gran's voice, I think of what she told me earlier today. "You have a wonderful opportunity to learn. You shouldn't waste it."

What did I learn from Addy? I ask myself as I pick up Grandpa's coin box. I learned that history is more than just dates. It's really the people who lived in the past and struggled to make changes. They're the ones who shaped the world we live in today.

I pass the bathroom where Danny's washing his face—and splashing water everywhere. I learned how much I like having a little brother. I put the box of coins down so that I can help Danny dry his hands and wipe up the counter. "Come on, Ducky. It's almost time for Dad's call."

Danny races into the living room ahead of me. I retrieve the box of coins and carry it to the living room, placing it on the floor next to the sofa.

"Grandpa, could you tell me more about great-great-granduncle Charley?" I ask.

Grandpa's whole face lights up. "Sure!" he says. He glances at the coin box, and then gives me a curious look. "That coin of his is really something, isn't it?" he says with a smile.

"Well, you're in a better mood all of a sudden," Gran says, coming in with a tray holding four cups. She's made coffee for herself and Grandpa, and I can smell hot chocolate for Danny and me. Gran sets the tray on the coffee table.

I'm so happy to see her, but I don't trust myself to say anything without crying. I just nod my head and give Gran a hug.

"You changed more than your clothes just now," Gran says, hugging me back. "Your whole attitude is different. What happened?"

Before I can answer, the laptop on the coffee table makes a beeping sound, and I know that Dad is about to Skype in. With one click, Dad's face is there. He's

grinning and doing a goofy wave.

I remember Addy waving good-bye. I wonder how long she had to wait before she saw her father again. I know that I won't ever take Dad's nightly call for granted, even if I have to say something that isn't easy.

I sit down between Grandpa and Danny. "Hi, Dad! I'm so glad to see you," I say, leaning toward the computer screen. I take a deep breath. "There's something I have to tell you."

☺ *The End* ☺

To read this story another way and see how different choices lead to a different ending, turn back to page 47.

A s soon as we're out the door, Addy starts telling me how wonderful school is and how much I'll love it. "My poppa wanted us to get to freedom so I could learn to read and write," she says. "That's why I'm working so hard in school. I want him to be real proud of me."

I think about my dad and how much he helps me with my homework. He's always telling me how proud he is of me when I do my best. That always makes me feel special. I imagine how disappointed he'll be when he hears about my social studies test.

All I can say to Addy is, "I hope I'll be as happy at school as you are."

We pass a storefront window, and Addy pauses. I read the hand-painted letters on the glass: *Delmonte's Secondhand Shop.* There are all kinds of items to look at: a big soup pot with a dented lid, a pair of socks with a small hole in one toe, three leather-bound books, an oval mirror on a stand.

"This is where Momma bought our dishes," Addy tells me. She points to a small, odd-looking lamp on display. It has a green base, but instead of a lampshade it has a tall glass top.

"That's the lamp Momma and me is saving up to buy," she says.

"But it doesn't even have a plug!" I say. Addy gives me a puzzled look.

"It's an oil lamp. The oil is kinda expensive, but Momma says a lamp will give us more light when I do my homework or when she has sewing to do."

I think about their cold, dark room and how hard it must have been for Addy's mother to sew by candle-light last night.

"But it takes a long time to save up three dollars!" Addy says.

"Three dollars?" I repeat. My allowance for one week is more than that! If it's taking them a long time to save three dollars, no wonder Addy only has one dress.

I'm wondering how much money Addy's mother earns at the dress shop when I notice two boys about our age hurrying out of a building carrying funny-looking brooms and clanking buckets. Their clothes and faces are covered with dark smudges. "What kind of school do they go to?" I ask.

Addy shakes her head. "They're not going to school.

They're going to clean chimneys," she says.

"But they're just kids!" I gasp. "Don't they *have* to go to school?"

Addy shrugs. "They have to work to help their families. Before me and Momma ran away, Uncle Solomon told me that freedom's got a cost. I didn't know what he meant, but now I do. Me and Momma got to buy everything in Philadelphia. Food. Clothes. Coal for the stove. It all cost money, and lots of kids work so their families have more money."

I dig into my pocket to touch the coin I have hidden there. "I didn't know that," I say. I think of Gran telling me how lucky I am to be able to go to school. Now I understand what she means.

☺ *Turn to page 40.*

ood morning, class," Miss Dunn says when she has everyone's attention. "Let's begin with a song."

Everyone stands up, and I wonder if we're going to sing the national anthem. Instead, the class sings a song that I don't know. The words remind me that I'm in another time.

> *We will welcome to our numbers*
> *the loyal, true and brave,*
> *shouting the battle cry of freedom.*
> *And although they may be poor,*
> *not a man shall be a slave,*
> *shouting the battle cry of freedom!*

Miss Dunn signals for us to take our seats, and then everyone recites the alphabet together. Hanging above the chalkboard in front of the room is a cloth banner with large letters printed on it. I read along with Addy and most of the other kids, but I can hear some of them making mistakes. Now I understand why Addy asked me if I knew my letters.

Next, Miss Dunn announces reading time. Addy

and I join a circle at the back of the room. We sit on old wooden crates, waiting for Miss Dunn to hand out the books. She gives one book to a girl in our circle and then moves on to the next group.

"Doesn't everyone get their own book?" I ask Addy.

She shakes her head. "We only have enough if we share."

The girl holds the book carefully, as if it's something very special. Most of the kids in my school don't give much thought to their books. Some people even lose them, or they turn them in at the end of the year with torn pages or water stains. I bet that doesn't happen here. Then I realize that if there are so few books, no one can take them home. That must really make it hard to study.

Before the girl starts to read, Addy whispers in my ear. "That's Fanny. She's smart. When she was on the plantation in Virginia, the master's daughter taught her to read and write." Addy is wide-eyed with wonder, but I hear fear in her voice, too. "Both of 'em could have gotten into a lot of trouble!"

I try to understand what Addy's saying. Slaves couldn't learn to read and write? White people who

taught them got punished for it? I'm too shocked to say anything. I think again about Gran telling me what a great opportunity I have to learn.

I listen as Fanny reads. The book is very easy—it's something Danny could read himself, and he's only five.

Addy's turn is next. She reads slowly, but she knows all the words. I can see that she's concentrating. It's clear that she wants to do well.

When Addy is done, she hands the book to me. "Do you want to try?" she asks gently. "I'll help you," she adds.

I bite my lip. I don't want to call attention to myself, and I certainly don't want to make Addy feel bad for not reading well. But I don't want to pretend that I can't read at all. What should I do?

☺ *To agree to read,*
turn to page 100.

☺ *To tell Addy you don't want to read,*
turn to page 98.

If I can't borrow a book, I'll have to buy one. But how? I don't have any money, except for great-great-granduncle Charley's two-cent piece, and I need that to get back home. I can't go and ask Mom or Dad to help me. I can't get to my secret stash of birthday money that's hidden in a shoe box in the back of my closet. But I have to figure out some way to get Addy a book.

Could I make her one? I know it wouldn't be as nice as the fancy leather-bound books we saw in Delmonte's store window this morning, but it would still be something she could read at home. I've never done anything like this before, so almost as soon as I get the idea, I'm wondering if I can really pull it off. But I can't give up. I know that's what Gran would tell me if she were here right now.

"And what are you thinking of so intently?" Miss Dunn asks. I hadn't even noticed that she was standing right in front of me. Before I answer, I look to see where Addy is. She and Sarah have gone back to their desks and are working on something on Sarah's slate.

"I'd like to give Addy a book," I whisper. "I know she loves reading."

Miss Dunn puts her hand on my shoulder. "That's a wonderful idea!" she says.

"I'm thinking about making one," I say, "but I don't really know how."

"That would certainly be very special for Addy," Miss Dunn agrees.

I nod. "Addy's going to teach her mother to read," I tell Miss Dunn.

"I'm not at all surprised," she replies. "Addy's quite determined to learn."

"She would be a great teacher," I say. "Look how she's helping Sarah. And she's helped me, that's for sure." That gives me an idea. "Miss Dunn," I ask, "how did you become a teacher?"

"I studied at the Institute for Colored Youth. It's a high school here in Philadelphia that trains colored people to become teachers."

"Do you think Addy could go there someday?" I ask hopefully.

Miss Dunn nods. "Addy has only been in school a short time, but she's a very bright student. She'll have to wait until she's eleven years old, and then pass exams in reading, writing, and mathematics to be accepted.

But I'm sure she would make a fine teacher one day."

That would be awesome! I think. Now I really want to help Addy. I know one book won't make her a teacher overnight, but it's a start.

I also know that Addy's family is the most important thing in the world to her. If she could get some news—any news—about where her father and brother might be, that would make her happy. I could help her write a letter to the freedmen's camps.

☺ *To make a book for Addy,*
   turn to page 115.

☺ *To help Addy write a letter,*
   turn to page 109.

Addy, I know my letters, but . . ." I pass the book to the boy beside me. "I don't think I want to read on my first day."

"It's all right," she says, patting my arm. "Miss Dunn says that's okay."

I feel relieved. We listen to the rest of the group. One or two of the students are confident, but the rest of them have trouble. Some only manage to get through a few words. But no one makes fun of them. In fact, several students help one another. I'm impressed that no one gives up.

After reading, we go back to our seats for a math lesson. Addy calls it arithmetic. She shows me some kind of counting tool with beads. "This is called an abacus," she tells me. It's a rectangular wooden frame with ten skinny rods running across it. Each rod holds ten beads.

Miss Dunn writes an addition problem on the chalkboard: 335 + 28. Addy's fingers move quickly as she moves the wooden beads from one position to another in the wooden frame.

"The bottom row is ones," Addy explains. "The next row is tens, and then the next is hundreds. On the top

is fives, fifties, and five hundreds."

I follow Addy as she moves two ten beads from the left to the right to count twenty, but then I'm lost.

Addy raises her hand. "It's three hundred sixty-three!" she says when Miss Dunn calls on her.

"That's correct," Miss Dunn says.

Addy passes me the abacus as Miss Dunn writes out a new problem on the board: 242 + 77. I stare down at the beads. Although I just watched Addy, I can't make sense of how to move the beads around. I can do the math in my head. The answer is 319. But I want to work it out the way everyone else is doing.

The girl named Harriet raises her hand and gives the right answer. Then she turns around and watches me as I continue to fumble with the beads. "Not every-one is as good at arithmetic as I am," she says.

The girl next to her snickers, and I feel my face grow hot with embarrassment. I want to shout, *Math is my best subject!* Instead, I stand up and run into the cloakroom.

☺ *Turn to page 104.*

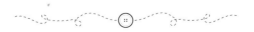

take a deep breath and look at the book in Addy's hands. "I'll give it a try," I say.

The book is easy, but I read very slowly. I don't want to show off, and I'm a little nervous about everyone watching me. After half a page, I pass the book on. Addy looks impressed.

"You read real good!" she whispers, her voice full of awe. I guess it's a big deal.

"I . . . I learned to read before I got to Philadelphia," I whisper back.

Addy looks like she's about to burst from happiness. "We can study after school together!"

Addy's enthusiasm makes me smile. Doing homework has never made me that excited.

When the next girl in our group begins to read, I glance around the busy classroom. There's a boy my age who is sitting at his desk. He's writing something, but it's what he's writing *on* that catches my eye. He's got two mini chalkboards, side by side, stitched together with some kind of cord. Each one of them is only about the size of the tablet I got for my birthday. I stretch my neck to watch. Several letters are neatly printed on one of the chalkboards. The boy is using

the other chalkboard to copy the letters. He's frowning with concentration. Even though he's moving his hand very carefully and slowly, his letters are wobbly. My little brother could do a better job printing.

Miss Dunn stops at his desk and looks over his shoulder. "Very good, Toby," she tells him. "You're showing so much improvement."

Toby smiles at the praise. I can tell that he's worked hard to earn it. That makes me think about how I've been at school lately. I've been so focused on missing my parents that there's been no room in my brain to focus on schoolwork.

I look back at Addy. She's not letting the fact that she misses her family stop her from being a good student. In fact, it seems to be the reason she's working so hard. Right now she's helping a girl in the reading group sound out a word. When the girl gets it, Addy gives her a huge congratulatory smile. Addy's not only doing her best, she's helping others do their best, too.

If Addy can put aside her worries and study, can't I?

☺ *Turn to page 106.*

hen Mrs. Walker comes back to the table, Addy says, "Momma, what do you think Esther's doing right now?"

"Right this very minute, Addy?"

"Right this very minute!" Addy winks at me.

"I think she's probably listening to a lullaby and falling asleep in Auntie Lula's arms." Mrs. Walker starts singing softly.

> *Hush, little baby, don't say a word,*
> *Momma's gonna buy you a mockin' bird.*

Addy joins in.

> *And if that mockin' bird don't sing,*
> *Momma's gonna buy you a diamond ring.*

I listen to their voices and think about my mom tucking me in every night. She still does, but now she does it after she gets home from school. I hear her drop her heavy book bag at the door, kick off her shoes, and tiptoe to my room. At the door, she whispers, "Yoo-hoo, moon!" That's because when I was little, I used to talk

to the moon in my sleep.

I turn to the window in the garret. "Moon," I whisper.

Addy stops singing. "What'd you say?"

"Mom," I say, trying not to cry. "I miss my mother."

"Of course you do, honey," Mrs. Walker says softly. "She misses you, too."

I close my eyes and listen to Addy and her mother sing the rest of the lullaby.

⊙ *Turn to page 30.*

plop down on the floor between the coats and shawls. All I want to do is hide.

Addy's right behind me. "Don't feel bad," she says, kneeling beside me. "You'll get better at it. That abacus is a funny contraption."

"I'm usually *good* at arithmetic," I tell Addy. *I'm usually good at school,* I think to myself. Suddenly it's the social studies test and not the abacus that has me upset.

"Then don't you listen to that Harriet! She thinks she's the best at everything. She's only the best at being Harriet." Addy smiles, and I can't help giggling.

"Come on back?" Addy stands up to leave.

But I shake my head. I'm kind of ashamed that I made such a dramatic scene over the abacus. I don't think I can face the rest of the class after that.

We hear skirts rustling, and Miss Dunn appears in the doorway. "Come, now," she says, crouching down in front of me. "Hasn't Addy convinced you to return to class?"

"No, ma'am. She won't budge," Addy says.

"This is your first day at school. There is no shame in not knowing something," Miss Dunn says gently.

I blink, remembering Addy telling me the same

thing at the church yesterday.

"Everyone is here to learn at their own pace," Miss Dunn continues. "Your job is to do the best you can."

That's the same thing Gran said when I told her about my social studies test. I sniff one last time and scramble up from the floor. "Can I try the abacus again?" I ask.

Miss Dunn stands up and nods. "Of course you can try again. You can always improve."

Addy loops her arm into mine, and we walk back to our desk together. *When I get back to my own school,* I think, *I'm going to try again with social studies. I know I can improve in that class, too.*

☺ *Turn to page 111.*

After we're done reading, it's time for geography. Addy and I join another small group, including Harriet and Sarah, in front of the big wall map. The map reminds me of social studies. Not my favorite. But when I take a closer look, I'm intrigued.

There's no North and South Dakota—just a big space labeled "Dakota Territory." And instead of Oklahoma, the state is called "Indian Territory." Up north, where Canada should be, are big letters that read "British America." When I find Alaska, it's labeled "Russian America." This is really interesting—even maps weren't the same in 1864.

"This is where we are," Addy says, putting her finger on the state marked Pennsylvania. Then she traces it down the map. "And this here's North Carolina, where Uncle Solomon, Aunt Lula, and Esther are," she says. She lets her finger drop. "Wonder where Poppa and Sam are?"

"My uncle is a soldier fighting for the Union army," Harriet pipes up. "I know that he's in Virginia, because he writes to us every week!"

Addy doesn't say anything and neither do Sarah or I. Harriet makes an impatient clucking sound and

turns to talk to someone else. The three of us look at the map again.

"Harriet thinks she's so special because she gets a letter every week," Sarah whispers.

"Harriet's lucky to know where her uncle is," Addy says quietly.

I feel a pang of guilt knowing where my father is.

"Addy, maybe your poppa and brother are traveling through one of the freedmen's camps somewhere right now," Sarah says.

"Could be," Addy replies hopefully. "Maybe they're on their way to Philadelphia right while we standing here talking."

"What's a freedmen's camp?" I ask.

"They a safe place for slaves to stay while they're traveling to freedom," Sarah answers. "People from the North give them food, let them rest, and help them get on to where they going."

"Addy," I say slowly, a plan forming in my mind. "Couldn't you send a letter to the freedmen's camp?" I ask. "Maybe somebody has information about your father and Sam."

"Maybe," Addy says. "But I don't write so good. I'm

not so sure I can write such an important letter."

"You mean, you can't write a letter like that *yet*," I correct her. "But you're working so hard that I know, someday very soon, you'll be able to do it."

"She right," Sarah says. "You already can read better than most of the students in our class!"

Addy's face lights up. "I love to read. I'm teaching Momma to read, too!"

I don't remember seeing a single book in the Walkers' room. Maybe I can give Addy a book she can take home. But how can I do it? I want to ask Miss Dunn, but she's talking to another student. Reluctantly, I turn to Harriet. "Where's the public library?" I ask quietly so that Addy doesn't hear. "I want to get a book."

Harriet raises her eyebrows. "Don't be silly!" she says. "The library doesn't let colored people borrow books!"

My mouth drops open. I want to shout, *That's ridiculous!* And then I remind myself that it is 1864.

☺ *Turn to page 95.*

I know what it's like to miss my dad, but I can't imagine how much worse I would feel if I didn't know where he was. I'm going to help Addy write that letter asking for information about her family.

After Addy and Sarah and I eat lunch together, I hang back from recess so that I can ask Miss Dunn for a pen and some paper.

"I'm afraid I have no paper to spare," Miss Dunn says. I blink in disbelief.

"But I only need a sheet or two," I say. Miss Dunn is shaking her head.

"Supplies are very limited, especially while the war is going on," she tells me.

"Th-Thank you, Miss Dunn," I stammer. I've heard teachers at my school talk about needing things like computers or projectors, but we always have paper.

Miss Dunn looks thoughtful. "Wait just a minute. I have some brown wrapping paper left over from a package I picked up yesterday," she says. "I can give you that."

I wonder if brown wrapping paper is right for an important letter like this, but I don't have a choice. I'll have to do the best I can.

Miss Dunn opens her desk and takes out a folded sheet. It's stiff and thick—like a grocery bag. She cuts a piece for me and hands me a pencil stub.

"Thank you," I say again, but I'm worried. Will the people at the freedmen's camp take this letter seriously when it's written in pencil on what looks like a paper bag? Then I have another worry. Where will Addy and I send this letter once it's written? From what Sarah said, there's more than one freedmen's camp. How will we know which is the right one?

☺ *Turn to page 118.*

ith Addy's help, I work with the abacus, and the rest of the morning goes quickly. At lunchtime, Addy and Sarah and I get our lunch pails and sit together inside the classroom. We find a spot beside one of the big windows where the sun is warm.

Addy's mother has packed us a cold meat pie to share and two apples. The crumbly pie is delicious, and my half is gone in a few bites. I'm almost done with my apple when Addy reaches into her lunch pail again.

"Look! Momma sent us a cookie." She pulls out one round cookie that's no bigger than the palm of my hand. Addy carefully breaks the cookie into three nearly equal pieces and hands one to each of us. I don't know anybody who shares as willingly as Addy.

"Mmm . . . ginger," Sarah says after she takes a bite. "These be good at the church benefit."

"Mmm-hmm," Addy mumbles through her mouthful. "Momma said I can help make some cookies to sell."

"You're as good at sewing as your Momma," Sarah says. "You oughta help on the quilt raffle!"

"What exactly is this benefit?" I ask.

"It's an event that will help us raise money for

people who are new to freedom," Addy explains. "People like us, and like the ones we meet on the pier yesterday."

I think of Addy and her mother arriving in Philadelphia with nothing. Where would they be if the church hadn't helped them? "I hope you raise a lot of money," I say.

"You mean you hope *we* raise a lot of money," Addy says. "You're gonna help, too, aren't you?"

"Sure!" I say, though I don't know what I can do to help.

We put the lunch pails away, grab our shawls, and follow the rest of the class outside for recess. A group of girls is gathered around someone who's jumping rope. It's Double Dutch. As we get closer, I can see that Harriet's the one who is jumping. The two ropes are turning furiously in different directions, but Harriet looks as if she's sailing between them. Her curls bounce up and down as she jumps.

"She's good," I say to Addy. Some of my friends can jump that fast, but I haven't quite gotten the swing of it. I can jump if the ropes aren't turning too fast.

"Want to jump?" Sarah asks me when Harriet stops.

"Addy and I will turn for you."

"Yes!" Harriet says. "Let's let the new girl try!"
She smiles brightly, and all the other girls turn to stare
at me.

I'm not sure about this, but Sarah and Addy give me
encouraging nods.

Just as Addy picks up her ends, Harriet rushes over
and grabs the ropes from Sarah. "I'll turn for her,"
Harriet says. "You're always too slow."

"Harriet!" Sarah protests, but Harriet starts turning,
and Addy has to join her.

I watch the moving ropes carefully, trying to find
the right time to start. I pause, weave, and then jump.
I'm in! I'm doing okay! I try to concentrate, but the
ropes start moving faster and faster.

"Slow down, Harriet!" Addy calls.

My boot catches one of the ropes, and I trip and
stumble to the ground.

"That's all right!" Addy says, helping me dust off
my dress. "The ropes were going too fast." She glares
at Harriet.

Harriet rolls her eyes at Addy. "Oh, you're just
making excuses for your pretend sister! It's too bad

you don't know where your *real* sister is!"

Addy opens her mouth to say something, but no words come out. Instead, tears fill her eyes.

☺ *Turn to page 55.*

iss Dunn, I'd really like to make a book for Addy," I say. "But I'm not quite sure how to do it."

"You're a good friend," Miss Dunn says. "I'll help you get started during recess."

After Addy, Sarah, and I eat lunch at our desks, we head to the cloakroom for our shawls so that we can go outside for recess. But Miss Dunn calls me back. Addy and Sarah pause at the door.

"You two can go on out. I need to ask your friend some questions for our records," Miss Dunn explains. Addy and Sarah leave, and Miss Dunn waves me over to her desk. "I can give you a pencil, but I don't have any writing paper."

No paper? I've heard of schools without computers, but never a school without paper. Miss Dunn sees my confusion, but she doesn't seem worried.

"Wait—I have the wrapping paper from the package I picked up yesterday," Miss Dunn exclaims. "I think that will work nicely."

Miss Dunn takes a large piece of heavy brown paper from her desk drawer. Then she gives me scissors and a ruler, and together we cut the brown paper into

squares that are all the same size. I don't see a stapler, so I'm not sure how I'm going to gather all these separate pages together into one book. When I ask Miss Dunn, she has a quick solution.

"Addy's mother is a dressmaker. I'm sure if you ask her, she'll let you use a needle and thread to bind the pages together."

"I didn't think of that," I say.

"Let me know if you need any other help," she tells me.

I go back to my desk, but I have to think for a moment before I start. I can't make any mistakes, since paper is so hard to find. Finally, I decide to write a short story about my friendship with Addy. First, I draw Addy and me at the church. I write *Freedom means meeting new friends*. Then I draw us at the table in the garret, and here at school, reading. Underneath each picture I write a few short sentences that Addy will be able to read.

I want to draw Addy's family, but I'm not sure what anybody except Mrs. Walker looks like. Addy doesn't have any photographs of her dad. I wonder if cameras even exist in 1864. I decide to just write the names of

Addy's family instead. At the top of the page, I write:

*Family is forever. Even if they are not here in
Philadelphia, they are with you in your heart.*

On the last page, I add a special message for Addy:

*Addy, you taught me how to have fun learning. Thank
you for being my friend.*

There. It's not perfect, but it's the best I can do with
the supplies I have. I hope Addy will like it!

☺ ***Turn to page 121.***

Before Addy and the others come in from recess, I tell Miss Dunn about the letter and ask her how I can get it to the right freedmen's camp.

"The Quaker Aid Society can help you," Miss Dunn assures me. "Take the letter to their office. Someone there will send it on."

That takes care of one problem. For the rest of the afternoon, I only half listen to the lessons as I wonder how I'm going to help Addy write a letter without the right supplies.

When the school day ends, Addy and I say good-bye to Sarah, who has to hurry home to help her mother. Addy and I set off for her house, walking briskly into the chilly afternoon wind.

"Addy, I want to help you write a letter to the freedmen's camps. Maybe they can help you find your father and Sam."

Addy's face brightens. "Oh! That would be mighty fine. If Mrs. Ford has any deliveries, I have to do those first, but then we can work on the letter!"

I'm happy that she's so excited. "But wait—there's a small problem," I explain. Miss Dunn gave me some paper, but it's kind of rough. And I don't have anything to write with. Do you have a pen at home?"

Addy shakes her head. "Me and Momma don't have use for a pen since I'm still learning to write. I only use my slate and slate pencil for practice. And besides, ink cost a lot of money." Addy pauses, and I can tell she's trying to figure out a solution. "Mrs. Ford!" she exclaims. "She might have a pen we could use. Let's go ask her." Addy and I practically run the rest of the way.

The dress shop is small and crowded with cloth, ribbons, and lace trimmings. Mrs. Walker is sitting at a long worktable, hemming a skirt by hand. An older white woman with wire-rimmed glasses is sitting near the window. She frowns at us when we burst inside. She doesn't look very friendly.

"Hello, Mrs. Ford!" Addy says cheerfully. "This is my new friend. We came straight from school. How many deliveries do you have for me today?"

"Thank you for being on time, Addy," Mrs. Ford says, her voice crisp but not unkind. "There are no errands or deliveries today. You and your friend are free to do as you please."

"That means there's plenty of time to study, girls," Mrs. Walker says, without looking up from her work.

"Yes, Momma," Addy says. "But first, Mrs. Ford, could we borrow your pen and some ink?"

Mrs. Ford raises her eyebrows. It looks as if she's going to say no, so I step forward. "I want to help Addy write a letter to the freedmen's camp. We're going to ask for information about her family," I explain.

Mrs. Walker's head jerks up. She looks at Addy with wide eyes. Addy smiles hopefully at her mother.

Mrs. Ford puts her sewing on the table. "That's very good of you," she says, standing up. She goes to a little desk in a corner and gets a pen and a bottle of ink. "Do you need paper?" she asks, holding a crisp sheet of smooth white paper.

I think about the rough brown paper Miss Dunn gave me. "Yes, please," I say. "Thank you."

I smile at Mrs. Ford when she hands me the paper, pen, and ink bottle. But my smile fades when I look closely at the pen. It's got a sharp, pointed edge. I've only seen an old-fashioned pen like this at a museum. I'm not sure I know how this pen works. Will I be able to help Addy after all?

☺ *Turn to page 127.*

S oon the class starts to file in from recess. I quickly roll up my pages, duck into the cloak-room, tuck the paper into a corner, and cover it with my shawl. I want to work a little more on my drawings, but I don't want Addy to see her surprise until it's finished.

The rest of the afternoon passes quickly as we study history and arithmetic. Miss Dunn ends the day with a grammar lesson.

"All right, class," she says. "Who can tell me what an adjective is?"

Lots of hands shoot up into the air, including mine.

"Sarah, can you tell us?" Miss Dunn asks as she writes the word "tall" on the big chalkboard in front of the room. Sarah frowns in concentration and then unhappily shakes her head.

In front of her, Harriet is pumping her hand up and down.

"Yes, Harriet?" Miss Dunn nods.

Harriet bounces out of her seat to stand beside her desk. "An adjective is a word that describes a noun," she answers. Then Harriet, in a singsong voice, decides to keep talking.

A noun is the name of anything,
A school or garden, hoop or swing.
Adjectives tell the kind of noun,
As great, small, pretty, white, or brown.

"Thank you, Harriet. That's very thorough," Miss Dunn says.

Harriet plops into her seat. She turns to Sarah and whispers, "Did you know that *smart* is an adjective, too, Sarah?" Sarah looks hurt.

"So is *nice*," I tell Harriet. "But you wouldn't know what that means."

"Leave Sarah be, Harriet!" Addy says with a sigh. Harriet just gives us a smug look and turns back to the front of the class.

☺ *Turn to page 130.*

Addy stays close to my side and helps me with the rest of the day's lessons. She works hard at every single subject. I'd get all A's if I worked as hard as Addy does!

When Miss Dunn dismisses us for the day, Addy, Sarah, and I walk home together.

"Did you like school?" Addy asks, swinging her school bag.

"I learned a lot," I say honestly. "For one thing, I learned what good students you and Sarah are!"

"Us?" Sarah asks.

"Yes, you two," I say.

"But we don't know all the answers," Addy protests.

"No, but you try so hard. You make me want to try harder, too," I say.

Addy smiles shyly at my compliment.

"Let's play some more Double Dutch," I suggest. "I could use the practice."

Sarah shakes her head. "Right now I got to work. My momma needs me to help with the laundry for her customers," she says.

"I've got to see if Mrs. Ford has any deliveries for me," Addy says. "The more tips I make, the closer

Momma and I are to buying our lamp."

"How much you got saved up?" Sarah asks.

"One dollar and thirty-four cents," Addy says cheerfully.

"That's good!" Sarah says encouragingly.

Addy nods. "But I'm hoping I can get done with deliveries early so that we can go to the church to help out with the benefit. Sarah, do you think you can come today?"

"I don't know," Sarah says. "Momma's been taking in extra wash 'cause we need the money. But I'll be there if I can!"

At the corner, Sarah waves good-bye and heads in the opposite direction. I wonder how she can be so cheerful about going home to do laundry.

"Sarah's very nice," I say to Addy as we head to the garret.

Addy nods. "Sarah was my first friend in freedom," she tells me. "And you're my second!"

"It must be hard for her to get her homework done when she has to work so much."

"It is," Addy agrees. "When Sarah and I get the chance, we do our lessons together."

I feel a twinge of guilt. All I have to do after school is study, but I'm not always eager to do it.

When we get to Addy's house, we don't go upstairs to the garret. Instead, we go to Mrs. Ford's shop on the first floor. It's a small, crowded space, full of long rolls of cloth, boxes of buttons, and baskets filled with thread, ribbons, and yarn. There's a squat black stove in the corner, but unlike the one upstairs, this one fills the room with heat. Addy's mother is sitting at a worktable in the back, bent over her sewing. She looks up and smiles when we come in. She glances at a clock on the wall and seems relieved to see us on time. *Just like my mom*, I think. *She'd be worried if we were late.*

There are two white women in the shop. One of them is wearing a fancy coat and hat, so she must be a customer. The other must be Mrs. Ford. Addy pulls me over to stand near the stove, putting a finger to her lips. We wait quietly until the customer leaves. At least it's toasty warm.

"Mrs. Ford," Addy's mother says, "this here is Addy's new friend. She just arrived in Philadelphia yesterday, and she's staying with us for a while."

Mrs. Ford takes off her glasses and gives me a long,

serious look. It makes me nervous. Will staying here cause trouble for the Walkers?

"Very well, Ruth," Mrs. Ford finally says, nodding her head. "As long as this child is as well behaved as Addy, I don't mind. But remember that I'm running a dress shop, not a hotel!"

"Yes ma'am," Mrs. Walker says quickly.

"Oh, thank you, Mrs. Ford!" Addy says happily.

I sigh with relief. The last thing I want to do is cause trouble for Addy or her mother.

☺ *Turn to page 132.*

A ddy and I go upstairs, where the afternoon sun is streaming through the garret window. The room is as cold as we left it this morning. But I don't even mind. I'm too focused on trying to help Addy.

"I'm not sure I know how to write with such a fancy pen," I confess as we sit down at the table.

"I've seen Mrs. Ford use it," Addy says. "It doesn't look too hard. But maybe you oughta practice before we start writing the letter," she suggests. "Where's the paper Miss Dunn gave you?"

We spread the brown paper on the table, and Addy shows me how to fill the pen with ink. I try to write something, but nothing comes out of the tip of the pen. When the ink finally does come out, it leaves a messy blob on the paper. My fingers are clumsy because it's cold in the room, and I'm getting ink splotches every-where. After practicing for nearly half an hour, my scratches on the brown paper finally start to look like letters. I've managed to figure out the pen!

"What should I write?" I ask as I carefully print the date at the top of the paper from Mrs. Ford.

Addy's leaning forward with her elbows on the table, watching me closely. "How about 'Dear Friends'?

Anybody who helps us is our friend, right?"

I write down "Dear Friends." Then I stop, waiting for Addy to tell me more. She's very quiet. When I look up, her face is sad.

"What if we don't get an answer?" she asks. "What if this war doesn't ever end? What if our family never gets back together? What if—"

I think about what my grandparents told me in the kitchen. "This is only temporary, Addy. You're going to get through this."

Addy sighs. "It just seem like forever since I laid eyes on Poppa and Sam."

"I know. But Addy, you still have a strong family, even if you aren't all in the same city," I say. I think of the e-mails I get from Dad and the notes Mom leaves for me on my nightstand when she gets home after I'm asleep. Even when I don't see my parents, they still let me know they're thinking of me. "Your poppa and brother are thinking of you all the time."

"Do you really think so?" she asks.

"I really do," I say. "Keep hope in your heart."

"All right," Addy says. "Let's write this letter!"

Addy thinks of the right things to say, and I write

her words carefully. When we're done, I read the letter aloud.

Dear Friends,

Please help me find my beloved family. I am looking for my father, Ben Walker, and my brother, Sam. Sam is around 17 years old. Both of them were sold from the Stevens Plantation, some 20 miles north of Raleigh, North Carolina. I would much appreciate any word on the two of them. I miss them very, very much.

Yours truly, Addy Walker

"That sounds good," Addy says, smiling with satisfaction. She blows softly across the page to help the ink dry.

I go to the washstand to scrub the ink off my fingers. "They're your words, Addy. I just wrote them down. Next time, *you're* the one who's going to do the writing."

☺ **Turn to page 133.**

fter the grammar lesson, Miss Dunn rings the bell and announces that class is dismissed. Addy, Sarah, and I wait until Harriet is out of the cloakroom to get our things. I tuck the pages of Addy's book under my shawl when Addy isn't looking.

On our way home from school, Addy loops her arm in Sarah's. "I can't stand it when Harriet is so mean to you," Addy says.

Sarah just shrugs. "I don't pay no mind to that Harriet. She just likes to hear herself talk."

"But it ain't right what Harriet said. You're the one who's been helping me ever since I came to freedom."

Sarah smiles. "I didn't do much, 'cause you were already smart when you got here."

"You're smart, too!" Addy insists. Sarah shakes her head.

"I could be, if I could study more. Helping Momma with her laundry work comes first, though."

"When do you do that, Sarah?" I ask.

"Before school. After school. Saturdays. Sometimes I stay home all day to help her. The more wash Momma takes in, the better. Even though my poppa's working, we need the money."

I can tell from Sarah's face that she wishes things could be different. I think about the kids we saw this morning, the ones who were going to jobs instead of school. They made me sad. I think about Gran telling me what a great opportunity I have to go to school. Now I really get it.

☺ *Turn to page 135.*

Addy," Mrs. Ford says, "we have two dress deliveries this afternoon. However, your mother has told me about the benefit at your church, and I understand there's work to be done there as well. I will make the deliveries on my way home if you would rather help with the benefit."

"That's mighty nice of you, Mrs. Ford," Addy says.

Mrs. Ford smiles. "Raising money to help families live in freedom is important work."

Addy turns to me. "You want to go with me to make deliveries up on Society Hill? Or should we go over to the church to help out?"

I'm not sure. Society Hill sounds fancy, and I know Addy counts on her tip money from this delivery job. But I also know how important the benefit is. Maybe we could be a bigger help at the church.

☺ *To make deliveries to Society Hill,*
   turn to page 142.

☺ *To help at the benefit,*
   turn to page 163.

hen my hands are dry, Addy and I go back down to the shop to return Mrs. Ford's pen and ink. Addy reads the letter aloud, and I can see tears in Mrs. Walker's eyes. "I'm real proud of you, Addy," she says.

"That is fine work!" Mrs. Ford says.

"Momma, can we take this to the Quaker Aid Society right now?" Addy asks. "They will know where to send the letter."

Mrs. Walker hesitates. "Yes," she finally says. "But please be careful. Especially after yesterday!"

"What happened yesterday?" Mrs. Ford asks.

"Addy and her friend got chased by a slave catcher," Mrs. Walker explains.

"He thought we were runaways," Addy adds.

Mrs. Ford's face turns red. "What an outrage!" she says. "Slavery is against the law in Pennsylvania. It should be against the law in every state!" I can tell that she's really upset, because the scissors she's holding are shaking.

"People are not property," she continues. "Every man and woman should have the freedom to make a good life for themselves and their families, no matter what color they are." Mrs. Ford takes a breath. "You take that letter, Addy. And I certainly hope one day very soon you'll be free to walk along any street in any part of our country without anyone stopping you."

When we leave the shop, I can't put Mrs. Ford's words out of my head. "Addy," I ask, "is freedom what you thought it would be?"

Addy shakes her head. "I thought freedom would be magic," she says. "In my dreams, we were all gonna be together in our own house, coming and going as we pleased. Momma and Poppa would earn lots of money, and we would have everything we wanted. All of us would learn to read and write, just like that!" She snaps her fingers.

"But freedom isn't like that," I say.

"Not yet," Addy says. "Freedom ain't magic. It's a lot of work."

I think of Grandpa, telling me to work hard to earn my freedom. Compared with Addy, I have so much freedom already.

☺ *Turn to page 145.*

A few blocks from school, Sarah says good-bye and heads off in the opposite direction. Addy and I walk the rest of the way to Addy's house without saying much. I'm lost in thoughts about my parents and how hard they both work to pay for all the things we need. I've never really thought about it before. The only "job" I have is going to school and doing my best. I understand that in a different way now. A wave of homesickness washes over me, and I sigh.

"You okay?" Addy asks.

"I miss my family," I say honestly.

Addy nods, and I can tell that she knows how I feel.

When we get to Addy's building, she takes me into the dress shop. A small bell over the door tinkles as we walk in. Addy's mother and a white woman are at a long worktable surrounded by cloth, pins, scissors, and thread. There's a small iron stove in the corner and several oil lamps in the room. The shop is warm and bright. Both women look up from their sewing when we come in.

Addy introduces me to Mrs. Ford, who looks at me over the tops of her wire-rimmed glasses. "Good day," she says briskly before turning to Addy.

"Addy, I need you to run some errands for me this afternoon."

"Yes, ma'am." Addy nods. "I'll just run to the privy first."

"That's fine," Mrs. Ford says.

Mrs. Ford goes back to her sewing, but Addy's mother looks at me and smiles. "How was your first day at school?" she asks.

"I learned a lot," I say truthfully. "And I got an idea. I'm making a book for Addy, as a gift."

Mrs. Walker smiles. She has dimples, just like Addy. "Addy's gonna like that."

"It's a surprise," I say. I know I need to talk fast, before Addy comes back, but I'm a little nervous asking for help.

"I did most of the work at school, but now I need to bind the pages together." I pause while I take the roll of papers from under my shawl and smooth them out on the worktable. "Could you help?" I ask shyly.

Mrs. Ford gets up to come and look.

"How thoughtful of you!" she says. "Ruth, don't we have some of that thin red ribbon left?"

The bell above the door jingles again. It's Addy!

Mrs. Walker tosses the dress she was working on over the brown pages. We all look in Addy's direction when she comes in.

Addy looks from one to another of us curiously.

"Addy," Mrs. Walker says, "you let your friend rest from her first day at school while you go on with your errands."

"That's a good idea," Mrs. Ford says. "These are for the post office," she says, giving Addy a stack of envelopes. "And these are the things I need at the dry goods store." She hands over a piece of paper with a list written on it.

"Yes, ma'am," Addy says, scanning the list. She looks at me. "I be back soon," she promises.

After Addy leaves, Mrs. Walker shows me how to thread a needle. Then she uses two scraps of cloth to show me how to make the stitches that will bind the pages together. I practice a few times on the cloth while she watches.

"That's right," Mrs. Walker says. "You'll do fine. Go on upstairs to finish."

I carry everything up to the garret. The little room is just as we left it this morning, which means cold.

Unlike the one in Mrs. Ford's shop, there's no fire in this stove. I keep my shawl on as I work. Step by step, I follow Mrs. Walker's directions, starting with threading the narrow ribbon through the eye of the needle. Sewing the heavy brown paper together is more difficult than working with cloth, and I poke my finger a couple of times with the needle. But I keep at it, and soon the pages are attached.

When the binding is done, I look at my drawings one last time, adding a few details. When I get to the page that says "Family Always," I stop to think of my own family. I miss them all, even Ducky Danny. Now that I know about Addy's family, I realize how close my family is, even if we're not together as much as we used to be. I also realize that I haven't been as hopeful as I could be. I'm going to change my attitude about a lot of things when I go home.

I hear the downstairs door open and close. In a moment, quick footsteps pound up the stairs. I hurry to hide my supplies and stand near the table with the book behind my back.

Addy opens the door gently. She's surprised to see me standing there. "I expected you to be lying down,"

she says. "How are you feeling?"

"I feel great, Addy. I have a surprise for you!"

I present the finished book to her with both hands. Addy is speechless. She holds it as if it's one of those fancy leather-bound books from Mr. Delmonte's shop. Slowly, Addy turns each page, her eyes growing wider.

"This is for me?" she asks in disbelief.

I nod. "Do you like it?"

"I love it," she says quietly. "It's my very own book. But I don't have anything to give you."

"You've already given me so much!" I say. "You helped me when I was all alone. You shared your home with me. Addy, you've been like a sister. Thank you for everything."

"I didn't do nothin' special," Addy says.

"Yes, you did," I insist. "You helped me see how strong my family really is. You've shown me that I can be strong, too."

Addy smiles and hugs me so tightly that it's hard to breathe. I really am grateful for her friendship, but right at this moment—more than anything—I want to be home.

"Addy," I whisper, "it's time for me to go."

"What?" Addy says, breaking away from our hug. "You're leaving?"

"I am," I nod. "My family's not coming to Philadelphia. I have to go to them."

"Do you have to go far?" Addy asks.

I think about the coin in my pocket. "Not too far," I answer. "But being with you and your mother makes me miss my mom. And my dad. And my brother and grandparents. I really want to be with them."

Addy nods slowly. "I understand," she says. "If you can get to your family, you got to." Addy sighs. "You're brave to do this alone."

I think of my grandparents and Danny waiting for me at home. I think of talking to Dad on the computer and waiting up for Mom to get back from class. My family *is* there for me. "I don't feel like I'm alone," I reassure Addy. "Not anymore." I touch her cowrie-shell necklace. "You've taught me that my family is with me all the time."

Addy looks surprised. "But I learned that from you!"

"I guess we learned it from each other," I say. "I'd like to say good-bye to your mom and to Mrs. Ford."

Addy nods. "And I want to show them my book. I can't wait to read it to Momma!"

As I follow Addy down the stairs, I feel hopeful. I hope that Addy's family is reunited. I hope that she goes on to become a teacher. Whatever happens, I know that Addy is strong. Now I feel strong, too. I know that I can adjust to the changes in my life and enjoy my family just as it is. *Hope is a powerful thing*, I think as I walk into the warm and sunny dress shop with my friend Addy.

☺ *The End* ☺

To read this story another way and see how different choices lead to a different ending, turn back to page 97.

have to admit that I'm curious to see Society Hill and get a glimpse of a fancy house. "Let's do the deliveries," I tell Addy.

Mrs. Ford hands each of us a large package wrapped in brown paper. I'm surprised at how much it weighs. But since women's dresses are so long, it makes sense that they would be heavy.

"Thanks for helping me," Addy says once we're on our way. "I like coming up here, but I get kind of lonely when I'm all by myself."

"After all the help you gave me in school today, I'm glad I can help you," I reply. "What's Society Hill like?"

"You'll see," Addy tells me, her eyes bright.

Boy, do I! The neighborhood is much cleaner and fancier than where Addy lives. Here, the streets are lined with trees and the iron lampposts have delicate scrollwork at the top. The row houses have tall windows surrounded by brightly painted shutters. Even the traffic is nicer. The horses are cleaner, and they're pulling elegant carriages, not rough wagons, along the quiet streets. It's clear that everyone who lives in this neighborhood is rich. I can't help comparing what I see here with Addy's simple home. How can

these neighborhoods be so close to each other and yet so different?

"Wow," I say to Addy as we pass a pair of well-dressed ladies on the sidewalk. "It's really fancy up here."

Addy looks up at one of the houses and nods. "It is like a dream to me," she says. "Back on the plantation, I imagined that freedom would mean living in a house like this."

I think about my house. I have my own room and a closet full of so many clothes that I never have to wear the same outfit two days in a row. I feel embarrassed about what I have compared with what Addy has.

"I used to lie next to Esther and dream of living on a street as pretty as this one," Addy continues. "But now, our family's not even in the same city!"

I hear the sadness in Addy's words. "But it *is* better here in Philadelphia, isn't it?" I ask.

"Oh, of course," Addy says quickly. "When we were on the plantation, we all got up before sunrise and worked till dark. It was hot out in the fields, and even when Sam and Poppa worked near me, I was always afraid of getting punished for talking to them."

I shudder. Addy shakes her head. "Freedom ain't perfect. Me and Momma still work hard, but Momma gets paid, and I get to go to school."

And what did I think freedom was? I ask myself. Walking to the ice cream shop with my friends. Avoiding the homework I'm not interested in. Addy's showing me that Grandpa was right. Freedom takes work.

☺ ***Turn to page 147.***

At the Quaker Meeting Hall, Addy and I make our way to a small office at the back of the large room. There are a lot of people there, so Addy and I have to wait. We sit on a long bench and watch men and women, and even a few children, take their turns asking questions or dropping off letters. Some of the women are crying as they leave.

"I didn't know so many families were separated!" I whisper to Addy.

Addy nods. "I only seen a handful of families come off the freedmen's boats together. Most everyone is missing somebody."

I think again about missing my dad and how differently I feel about our separation now that I've met Addy and understand what real separation is. I still miss him, but I know where he is. I know he's safe. And the rest of my family is together.

"Next?" A white man with thick, curly blond hair waves us forward pleasantly. "Hello. I'm Mr. Cooper."

Addy hands him her letter. He reads it silently. When he looks up, his face is serious, but still kind.

"Which of you is Addy?"

"Me." Addy's voice sounds small.

"We'll pass this letter along, Addy. It takes time to get an answer, but we'll do our best to help you."

"Thank you, sir. My momma and I are gonna keep hoping."

Mr. Cooper nods. "That's the best thing you can do. We never know when good things are going to happen. Why, just recently I met a man who found his family after walking six hundred miles!"

I'm stunned. I think of how long it took us to drive from Tennessee to Florida for vacation. Dad said it was a little over six hundred miles, and it took us nine hours in a car! It would take years to *walk* that far!

"My poppa would walk six hundred miles and then some, to find us!" Addy says.

Mr. Cooper laughs. "Nothing can separate a family's love. You girls check back with me in a few weeks. We'll see what we know."

"Yes, sir," Addy says. "We will!"

Nothing can separate a family's love. Hearing those words gives me a funny feeling. I think it's time to join my own family again.

☺ *Turn to page 149.*

ere's the first address," Addy says, climbing the steps. The brass knocker on the door is shaped like a lion. She raps the knocker against the door three times.

"What if nobody's home?" I ask.

Addy shakes her head. "The maids are always home," she says.

Sure enough, the door swings open. A black woman wearing a dark uniform and an apron looks at us. "Yes?" She sounds as if she's asking a question and answering one at the same time.

"We from Mrs. Ford's dress shop," Addy tells her in a very grown-up voice. "With a delivery."

"Ah." The maid opens the door a little wider so that we can step in. She takes the package and then looks us up and down as if she's not sure she can trust us alone inside the house.

"Wait here." Her boots click on the polished floor as she walks away. The entrance hall is bigger than Addy's room above Mrs. Ford's shop.

Addy tilts her head toward a room on the left. "Take a look in there," she says. I lean over her shoulder for a better view.

The room is fancier than any I've ever seen. Gold-framed mirrors hang on the walls, and the tall windows are draped with dark curtains tied back with gold ropes. It looks as though dragons are curled in the pattern of the huge rug. I can see the edge of a red sofa with skinny, curved legs.

The maid returns and hands Addy five pennies. Without a word, she opens the door and waves us out into the cold.

When the door closes behind us, Addy grins and drops the pennies into a little cloth purse underneath her shawl. "We five cents closer to our lamp," she says happily.

"That's wonderful," I say, trying to match Addy's enthusiasm. But it's going to take her a lot of pennies, and a very long time, to earn three dollars.

☺ *Turn to page 151.*

ddy almost dances along the sidewalk. She's so encouraged by Mr. Cooper's story! But all I can think about is the fact that I'm separated from my family by more than six hundred miles—it's over a hundred and fifty years! Suddenly I'm missing all of them like crazy. I don't even care anymore about taking the consequences for my bad grade. Being with my family is more important. My fingers curl around the coin in my pocket.

"Addy, I have to find my family," I suddenly blurt out.

Addy stops and turns to me. "Of course you do," she says. "Your heart is where your family is."

I can't answer at first without my voice wavering. I swallow. This is hard.

"My family has a meeting place like yours does, but it's not Philadelphia. I need to keep going. I need to go today."

"Right now?" Addy asks. She looks surprised, but she nods. She understands. Addy takes my hand. "You're gonna find them. I know it!"

"I'll never forget everything you and your momma have done to help me," I say. "I really mean it."

"I never would have written that letter without you," Addy says.

"Yes, you would have," I assure her. "But I'm glad I could help. Good luck!"

Addy smiles. "We don't need luck. We have hope!" We hug each other. "I'm gonna miss you," she whispers.

"I'll miss you, too. Good-bye, Addy!"

☺ *Turn to page 32.*

Back on the sidewalk, Addy and I pick up our pace. Dark clouds block the sun, and the air feels much colder. The wind picks up, too.

At the second house, a cheerful young woman answers the door. "Oh, you have the Missus's gown!" she says, shivering in the cold. "Follow me to the kitchen. You can warm yourselves by the stove for a moment."

Addy and I follow the woman across a wide hall, through a door, and down a narrow staircase. I look over my shoulder at Addy, whose face is full of excitement. I don't think she's ever been any farther than an entrance hall in a house like this.

I can smell the food before we even get to the kitchen, and my stomach growls hungrily. I usually have a snack when I get home from school, but Addy and I haven't eaten since lunch.

At the bottom of the stairs, the maid leads us down a short hallway and into a kitchen unlike any I've ever seen. "Wait here where it's warm," she says, leaving us standing with our mouths open.

There's a long table down the center of the room, and it's covered with food. There's a whole chicken

and an enormous ham, both steaming from the oven.
A shiny silver fish lies on a cutting board, its head still
attached. Baskets overflow with fruits and vegetables,
potatoes and onions. On another table I count five
frosted cakes next to a tray of beautifully decorated
pastries. Everything smells delicious.

"This is more food than we had at the church
yesterday!" Addy says. I can tell she's amazed. I
am, too.

Four women wearing caps and long aprons hurry
around. I can't believe they don't bump into one
another as they move pots and bowls, stirring and
slicing. A giant black stove fills almost one whole wall,
and another woman stands in front of it, tending the
half dozen pots that boil and bubble. There's a deep
sink on one end of the kitchen, with a pump next to it.
I guess no one has to go outside to get water, like Addy
does.

"All this is for one family?" I whisper.

Addy is speechless, so she only nods.

The nice maid is suddenly back—she must have
come through a different door. She picks something up
as she passes the long table.

"Here's something for your trouble," she says, handing each of us three pennies. "And here's a bit of bread. These rolls got burned, so they're not fit to serve at dinner. "

The roll is warm in my hands. Without thinking, I take a bite. It's delicious.

"Thank you!" Addy says.

"Thk—oo!" I mumble, my mouth full of bread.

The maid laughs as she leads us up a different set of stairs and lets us out the back door. We're in the alley, but even this part of Society Hill looks clean and fancy.

☺ *Turn to page 157.*

'm not leaving!" I say firmly, pulling Addy to a corner of the theater.

"Then I guess I'm not, either!" Addy says.

We stay where it's dark and find a spot behind a curtain. We can see most of the show, and we can hear everything just fine. The show is funny, full of jokes and riddles. We keep covering our mouths to keep anyone from hearing us laugh.

When the show is over, we slip out of the theater before everyone else. "My brother Sam can always make me laugh," Addy says as we hurry home against the chill. "He tells riddles, too. Like this one: 'What's gotta be broken before you use it?'"

"I don't know." I shrug.

Addy can hardly keep from giggling. "It's an egg!"

We're on the street now, so I can laugh out loud. "Sam's riddles are good! I have to remember that one so I can tell Danny when I see him again." All of a sudden, I miss Danny.

"I miss Sam," Addy says, her laughs fading. "I wonder where he is."

"You said he and your poppa got sold. Do you think they're still in North Carolina?" I ask.

Addy shakes her head. "I know Sam ran away—
especially after Poppa told him that we were all comin'
to Philadelphia. He may be on his way here. But he
may have joined the army. He always talked up becom-
ing a soldier, so he could fight for freedom." Addy and
I wait for a wagon to pass before we cross the street.
"I'm scared for him," Addy admits. "Running away is
dangerous, but if he's a soldier, he could get killed."

"You said Sam is stubborn. It sounds like if he
wants to be a soldier, nothing's going to stop him,"
I say.

Addy sighs. "You're right."

We walk a while in silence. The late afternoon sun
is slipping away. I watch a man light a streetlamp with
a flame on a long stick.

"You know what I just realized?" Addy says.

"What?"

"We saw the whole puppet show. We didn't let that
woman stop us!"

I grin. "We didn't give up!"

"I'm not gonna give up on my family getting
back together, either," Addy says with determination.
"Poppa and Sam will get to Philadelphia, and then

Poppa will go back to the plantation for Esther, Auntie Lula, and Uncle Solomon."

"Good for you, Addy."

"I know you miss your family, too," Addy says gently.

I think of Danny again, and my grandparents. I *do* miss them.

"Remember, you have to have hope and be patient. That's what Momma says."

Hope. The word sparks something in my brain. When we first met, Addy told me about the Quaker Aid Society helping folks keep hope alive. "Addy, I have an idea," I say. "If your poppa and Sam are on their way to Philadelphia, they may have gotten help along the way. Maybe someone at the Quaker Aid Society can find out where they are!"

"You think so?" Addy asks, her eyes sparkling with excitement.

"There's nothing wrong with asking," I say.

"Let's go!" Addy says.

☺ *Turn to page 166.*

ddy and I stand in the alley for a few minutes eating our bread. "This doesn't taste burned to me," I say, finishing my roll.

Addy shakes her head as she takes small bites and chews slowly. She's going to make her bread last.

"I never saw a kitchen like that before," I say.

"Me either," Addy agrees. "It was even bigger than the one on the plantation, and that was pretty big. I used to help my Auntie Lula in there sometimes."

"Did you like working in the kitchen?" I ask, thinking of cooking with my mom or my grandpa. They both make it fun to help, and I like tasting everything they make.

"I liked working with Auntie Lula," Addy says with a faraway look in her eyes. "Sometimes she put aside some scraps for me, and we could talk while we were cleaning up. But most of the time I was in the dining room, standing in the corner while Master Stevens's family ate."

"You just stood there?" I ask.

Addy nods. "Until I had to pour a glass of water or get someone more soup. It's real hard to smell all that food when you're hungry." Addy finishes her bread.

"Let's go home," she says, walking ahead of me and out of the alley.

When we reach the sidewalk, I try to give Addy my three pennies. "I didn't do anything to earn this," I tell her. "I want you to have it."

"No!" Addy wraps my fingers around the money in my palm. "You need it as much as Momma and I do. Besides, it's been so much fun having you along with me!"

I remember Addy telling me how lonely she gets making deliveries. I think of Gran chatting with me while I unload the dishwasher, and that makes me smile. "Having someone to talk to always makes work go faster, doesn't it?"

"It sure does," Addy agrees.

"Listen, Addy. Please take the money. You and your mother have helped me so much. Won't you let me add this to your lamp fund?"

"Well . . ." She hesitates for a moment longer, but then when I open my hand, she takes the coins and puts them away with the others.

"This a big day," she says happily. "Eleven cents *and* a warm roll!"

I laugh with Addy. As we head back to Mrs. Ford's shop, I wish that I could add Grandpa's coin to Addy's savings. But I know that's impossible. It's my only way home.

☺ *Turn to page 34.*

Addy looks as if she's too nervous to enjoy the puppet show, even if we can avoid the woman with the hat. I think of our experience with the slave catcher, and I realize that things could get out of control.

"Let's skip the puppet show this time," I say. "Let's go see Sarah instead!" Addy looks relieved.

When we get to Sarah's, I expect to go inside the building. Instead, Addy leads me down a narrow passage to an alley that's even darker and smellier than the one behind her building. We step around piles of trash, and I hold my nose as we pass the privy.

There are clotheslines strung back and forth across the alley. It takes me a minute to spot Sarah in the dim light. She's standing on her toes, stretching up to remove a pair of pants. Dozens and dozens of shirts, pants, and skirts hang from the line, which is almost too high for Sarah to reach. *How does anything dry in this cold air?* I wonder with a shiver.

As Addy and I make our way down the alley, I step in a dirty puddle. Water leaks into a hole in my boot, and I cry out. The sound makes Sarah stop her work. "Who that comin'?" she calls, her voice edged with fear.

"It's me," Addy calls.

"Hey, Addy!" Sarah says, sounding relieved. "You both here!" she says happily when she sees me.

The front of Sarah's coat is sopping wet, and her hands look red and chapped from handling the wet clothes. She must be freezing!

"We only had two deliveries, so we got done fast," Addy explains. "We were hoping you were finished, too, and could do some Double Dutch with us."

"That sounds like fun, but I can't," Sarah says. "My momma and I have to finish a big order. After I take in this load, I got to start the ironing. There's still more to wash, so I won't be at school tomorrow."

"You sure?" Addy sounds wistful.

Sarah drops her head. "Yeah."

"I'll bring the lessons by after school. Maybe then you'll have time to study?" Addy says hopefully.

"Maybe," Sarah says uncertainly.

"All right, then." Addy looks sad. "See you tomorrow."

"Bye!" I say.

"See y'all," Sarah says, turning back to the laundry.

"Does Sarah always work back here by herself?"

I ask as we make our way out of the dim alley.

Addy nods. "It's a hard job. For the washin', Sarah's got to boil the clothes in big cauldrons. It gets awful hot and steamy in the summer. This time of year, though, Sarah's hands freeze."

I think of our washing machine at home. I really can't imagine having to *boil* laundry.

"You know, Sarah might not stay in school too much longer," Addy says sadly as we head back to her house.

I can't believe it. "What do you mean?"

"In freedom," Addy explains, "everything costs money. Sometimes everybody in a family has to work so there's enough. That's how it is for Sarah."

I don't know what to say. I don't always like to study, but I would never have to make a choice between studying and working to help my family.

"Sometimes," Addy says, "I think about it, too."

Wait. *Addy's* thinking of dropping out of school?

☺ *Turn to page 165.*

think about Mrs. Ford's words: *Raising money to help families live in freedom is important work.* "I'd like to help at the church," I tell Addy.

Addy claps her hands in excitement. "Me, too!" she says, turning to her mother. "Momma, can we go right now?"

Mrs. Walker nods. "Be careful on your walk. I'll be there soon."

Addy and I hurry to the church. The meeting hall is even more crowded than it was yesterday when I arrived with the other newcomers from the pier. A steady hum of voices, and an occasional shout, fills the room. Men, women, and children rush about, yet everything seems organized. I can feel the excitement.

"There's so much going on!" I say, looking around. "Where should we help?" Before Addy can answer me, some boys bump past us, laughing and carrying crates of food toward the kitchen in the back of the hall.

At the other end of the hall, a woman's voice calls out over the noise. "I want to thank you all for coming to help this afternoon!" she says.

"That's Mrs. Drake, the Reverend's wife," Addy says. The noise dies down as people stop to listen.

"If you haven't found a way to help yet, we have committees for everything from refreshments to decorating. And we will have a quilt raffle, so we'll need lots of volunteers to make squares!"

A chorus of approval ripples around the room. Addy looks excited.

"If you'd like to make a square, come to the quilting table," Mrs. Drake says. I see several women and girls move in that direction.

"Let's make a quilt square!" Addy suggests, pulling me toward Mrs. Drake.

"I want to help," I say, "but I don't know how to sew a single stitch—remember?"

"I'll teach you," Addy offers. "It will be fun!" she says enthusiastically.

I don't feel very confident in my sewing skills, but Addy looks so eager that I can't say no.

☺ *Turn to page 168.*

But you love school!" I say to Addy. I can't believe what I'm hearing. Miss Dunn even thinks Addy could be a teacher someday. "You can't leave school!"

"Well, I don't want to, but I been thinking. I could help Momma—and all my family—so much more if I worked full-time. I could earn more delivery tips, and maybe get another job, too. Me and Momma could get that lamp, and Momma could sew at night."

"But Addy, isn't that lamp going to help you do your homework?"

Addy sighs. "I know. But maybe right now it would be better if I worked. I can go to school later."

I cannot let this happen. I'm trying to figure out how to convince Addy when I realize we're back at Mrs. Ford's. The dress shop is dark.

"Don't say anything to Momma," Addy says before we head to the garret. "I don't want to upset her."

Then don't do this! I think as I follow Addy up the steps.

☺ *Turn to page 172.*

A ddy knows the way to the Quaker Meeting Hall. We hurry, hoping someone will be there even though it's getting late and the shops we pass are closing for the night. When we get to the hall, there's a light shining from a room in the back. A man sits at a desk piled with papers. He looks up and smiles when we come into the room.

"What can I do for you girls?" he asks kindly.

I thought I might have to give Addy a nudge, but she walks right up to the desk and starts talking. "I'm Addy Walker, and I'm trying to find my poppa, Ben Walker. He was sold from the Stevens plantation in North Carolina. I'm looking for my brother, too—his name is Sam Walker. He was sold with my poppa." Addy's words rush out in a hurry. "I'm hoping you might find out if they've been to any freedmen's camps and if they're on their way to Philadelphia yet."

I watch the man write down the details of what Addy has told him.

"I can make inquiries with a few aid societies between North Carolina and Pennsylvania on your behalf. These things take time, but perhaps I can help you get some information about your family."

My heart skips a beat. He's going to help! I squeeze Addy's hand.

"You stop in and see me in a few weeks. My name is Mr. Cooper."

"Thank you, Mr. Cooper," Addy says. "I'll be back!"

As we leave the meeting hall, Addy is the happiest I've ever seen her.

"I can't wait to tell Momma!" She's almost shouting in the street. "You was right to ask for help!" She stops. "Wait—what about your family? We should go back and have Mr. Cooper ask about them, too!"

I don't want Mr. Cooper to spend time looking for people he won't find—not when I know perfectly well how to get to my family myself. The truth is, all this talk about reuniting Addy's family makes me miss mine. I know it's time for me to go home.

☺ *Turn to page 24.*

Addy and I make our way to the table where Mrs. Drake is standing. It looks like the work-table in Mrs. Ford's shop. There are baskets filled with spools of colored thread, scissors, and brightly printed cloth. Some women are cutting large squares of white cloth. Other women and children are already working, sewing different designs onto the squares.

I look over their shoulders at the neat stitching while Addy gathers our supplies. She leads me to a spot at the table. We each have a square with a cloth flower pinned on it. There are five petals around a round center.

"I'll help you thread your needle," Addy says.

I feel a bit foolish. I should have tried harder when Mom tried to teach me to sew.

"Now we sew the petals to the square. We're gonna use the blanket stitch." Addy shows me a basic stitch. It's simple, but my work looks pretty sloppy compared with her small, even stitches. I go slowly, remembering what Gran said about my schoolwork: *Just do your best.* Addy is quietly concentrating, and so am I.

"This quilt is sure to bring in a lot of money," a young woman on the other side of the table says. I

glance at her square and see a complicated design taking shape. Then I look at my square. The flower looks crooked.

The girl next to her says, "Some of the money will go to buy supplies for the hospitals that treat wounded soldiers. My brother Rafe is fighting for the Union."

An older woman talks without looking up from her work. "Some of the money will help widows and orphans, too."

"We all have to work hard to make this quilt something beautiful," the first young woman says. "Every dollar we raise will go toward helping free colored people. We have to make this whole event a big success!"

I look at Addy. She's beaming, pleased to be part of this group.

I'm struck by just how important this benefit is. This money isn't for a sports team or a class trip to an amusement park. It's to help make real people's lives better! I look down at my square. The thread is bunched up, and one of the petals is hanging over the edge of the square. How did that happen? My square isn't good enough to be part of this quilt—not if someone's going to pay a lot of money for it. I can't let my square ruin the whole project.

I'm about to say something to Addy when Mrs. Drake approaches the table. She puts her hand on Addy's shoulder. Quickly, I fold my square so that Mrs. Drake can't see the mess I've made.

"Addy," she says, "can you please help me sort some of the cloth that Mrs. Ford donated? I only need you for a few minutes."

"Yes, ma'am!" Addy hops up. "You keep on working," she tells me. "I be back soon as I can!"

I look down at my square. Is it even worth working on it anymore? I look up to watch Addy disappear into the crowded hall with Mrs. Drake. That's when I spot a bin full of rags across the room. Next to the bin, there's a man making rugs from the rags and scraps of fabric. Maybe that would be a better use for my botched quilt square.

The women and girls who are sewing don't seem to notice me easing up from the worktable and strolling across the room. I see Mrs. Walker coming into the hall. She stops to hang up her coat and hat. I step closer to the rag bin. Should I just toss my square into the bin?

Or should I wait until Addy gets back and show her my mess? I don't think there's any way to fix the square, but maybe Addy will have an idea.

*To show the square to Addy,
turn to page 174.*

*To toss the square in the rag bin,
go online to* **beforever.com/endings**

hen we walk into the garret, the stove is lit and the candle is flickering on the table. The room feels warm after the chill of the afternoon. Addy and I take off our hats and shawls, and I notice that there are three chairs at the table. Addy notices too.

"Momma, where'd that other chair come from?"

"Mrs. Ford let me bring one up from the shop since we have a guest," Mrs. Walker answers. "Sit down and rest a minute after your errands." Mrs. Walker asks us about the afternoon as she begins to prepare supper at the table.

"We saw the biggest kitchen in the world, Momma!" Addy begins. As Addy describes the afternoon, her mother listens, asking questions and exclaiming over the fancy houses that are so different from the nearly empty room we're sitting in now.

I don't say very much. It's fun to listen to Addy and her mother talk. It reminds me of the conversations at my house, before Mom went back to school and Dad started his job out of town. At dinnertime, I'd help Mom make her special taco salad, or help Dad cook his famous turkey burgers, and I would tell them all about my day. I really miss that.

But wait. Aren't Gran and Grandpa there now, cooking and listening? My family has changed, but the love hasn't. Mom and Dad still listen to me talk about my day. But now it's *after* dinner, when Dad calls or Mom gets home from class. I think I finally understand that that hasn't changed. Now Gran and Grandpa are there, too. The only person who isn't letting that be fun is me.

"Girls, how 'bout you wash up and help me make the biscuits?" Mrs. Walker says.

"My mom makes special biscuits at Thanksgiving," I tell Mrs. Walker as Addy and I go to the washstand.

Mrs. Walker nods and smiles. "In our family, we give thanks every day!"

I know that when I go back to my home, I will from now on, too.

☺ *Turn to page 178.*

I should talk to Addy before I just quit. As I turn back to the quilting table, I see Mrs. Walker heading in my direction. She's smiling until she sees the look on my face.

"What's wrong?" she asks.

I hand her my square. "It's a disaster," I say.

Mrs. Walker takes the wrinkled mess from my hands but keeps her eyes on me. "Is this the first time you've sewn a quilt square?"

I nod my head shyly.

"Well then, how can you expect it to be perfect the first time?" she asks gently. "You may need a little bit of help, but mostly you need to keep trying. Practice will make you better." She hands the quilt square back to me. I think of social studies and how if I'd studied steadily, I wouldn't have failed the test. I guess I needed more practice there, too.

"I just don't want my sloppy square to ruin the whole quilt," I explain. "It won't make as much money."

"I don't think you need to worry about that," Mrs. Walker says. "Everybody knows this quilt is a story about the people who made it—about their journey to freedom. Gettin' here wasn't perfect, either.

But we're here. That's what matters. That's what people are gonna see in this quilt."

Suddenly Addy is by my side. "Hi, Momma!" she says happily. Then she looks at me. "Finished already?" she asks.

"Actually, I was about to give up," I say.

"Let me see," Addy says. She doesn't laugh at my terrible job.

"Do you want to give up?" Addy asks.

"No," I say. "But will you help me?"

"Of course!" Addy says brightly.

Mrs. Walker smiles. "I be over at the quilting frame if you girls need me," she says, giving my shoulder a squeeze.

Addy and I sit down at the table again. "We'll pick it all out and start over."

"You can do that?" I ask.

"Sure you can," Addy says. She shows me how to pull the thread from the back of the square to remove the crooked flower. Then she hands it back to me.

"When me and Momma come to Philadelphia, we had to start over," Addy explains as she watches me work slowly to untangle my mess. "Just about everyone in this room had to pull up their roots and start fresh here in freedom. That's kinda like pulling out threads and starting over." Addy picks up her own quilt square and keeps working on her flower.

"I never thought about it that way," I say. If Addy's family—and all these people around us—can start over, then I can, too. On my quilt square, on my schoolwork, and on my attitude with my family.

After about an hour, Addy is nearly done with her square. I only have three of my five petals sewn down, but I'm proud of what I've done.

Addy is, too. "You did a good job," she says. "Let's put our squares in Momma's bag. We can finish them at home and bring them back tomorrow."

We find Addy's mother in a corner of the hall where some men and women are putting long pieces of wood together.

"What's that?" I ask.

"It's the quilt frame," Addy tells me. "After all our squares get pieced together into one big square, it gets stretched over that frame along with the lining. Then we stitch right through all the layers in fancy patterns to sew the top and bottom together. That's quilting."

"All the little squares fit together into one big square," I repeat. "That's kind of like each of these people, coming from different places and helping out with the benefit, right?"

"You right," Addy says. "Nobody can do this all by themselves. Everybody works together to help one another. Reverend Drake calls that *community*."

I think about how my parents and grandparents work together for our family. When I go home, I know I'm going to be a stronger part of that community. I'll start again, and this time I'll do a better job studying and finishing my chores and being patient while our family's separated. Being with Addy has taught me how to do that.

☺ *The End* ☺

To read this story another way and see how different choices lead to a different ending, turn back to page 132.

A fter a simple supper, the three of us sit at the table. Mrs. Walker sews, and Addy and I do schoolwork. Addy's writing words on her slate for me to read. I pause each time she writes a new word—not because I don't know the word but because it's hard to see by the light of only one candle. Each time a draft blows across the room from the window, the candle flickers, threatening to go out. I can see why the Walkers need a lamp.

I haven't stopped thinking about our conversation about Addy's quitting school. I know she doesn't want to, and I know her mother wouldn't want her to, either. How can I bring that up? Then I have an idea.

"Addy, would you read these words for me?" I ask. "I want to make sure I'm saying them correctly."

"Sure," Addy agrees. She reads the list easily.

"You're such a good reader," I tell her, glancing at Addy's mother.

"She sure is!" Mrs. Walker agrees. "Her poppa gonna be so proud of her when he sees her reading and writing. More than anything, he wanted Addy to go to school in freedom."

I glance at Addy. I can tell she's thinking about our

conversation now, too. "Imagine," I say. "You can teach Esther her letters when she gets to Philadelphia. With your help, Addy, she'll be able to read before she even goes to school."

"Won't that be something!" Mrs. Walker says. She gets up to stoke the last of the coals in the stove. "First Addy gonna teach me to read, and then she gonna teach Esther. I'm so proud of you, honey."

Addy leans close and whispers so that her mother can't hear. "Okay," she says, smiling slowly. "I won't leave school. I've got a job to do right here in my family."

I smile and breathe a sigh of relief. That's what I wanted her to say!

☺ *Turn to page 102.*

ABOUT Addy's Time

When Addy and Momma first arrived in Philadelphia in 1864, they wondered if the big, crowded city could ever feel like home. This was where freedom was, Poppa had said. Addy wanted so much to believe him, but she soon discovered that the reality of freedom was very different from what she'd dreamed it would be.

Although slavery had been outlawed in the North since the early 1800s, people who lived in northern states were *segregated*, or kept separate, because of the color of their skin. Addy and Momma were not free to shop in some stores, attend some cultural events, or even live where they wanted.

Although Addy was free to get an education, she had to go to a school that was for black children only. Schools for black children generally had fewer supplies and worse building conditions compared with those for white children. Children weren't required by law to go to school, but many former slaves were eager to learn and attended for at least a few years. Girls and boys usually stopped going to school after the age of 12 or 13, though many students had to stop when they were even younger in order to help their families earn money. By the time Addy was in school, thousands of African Americans had learned to read and write. They knew that education meant true freedom—that education opened the door to better jobs and better lives.

Many *freedmen*, or newly freed and escaped slaves,

started new lives in large northern cities, such as New York, Philadelphia, Cincinnati, and Boston. Like Addy and her mother, most people turned to an African American church for help when they first arrived. Church members, many former slaves themselves, welcomed newcomers with food, clothing, and help adjusting to their lives as free people. Most northern cities also had freedmen's aid societies, and Philadelphia alone had more than a hundred. Organized and operated by the black community, aid societies helped thousands of families each year find homes and jobs. People like the Walkers were grateful not only for the help they received but for the friendship they found at these churches and aid societies.

One important group in Philadelphia was the Quaker Aid Society. A white religious organization, the Quakers were *abolitionists*, or people who opposed slavery. In addition to helping freedmen find their families, the Quakers founded the Institute for Colored Youth in 1837. The I.C.Y. was the first high school for African Americans, and it was one of the few schools in America where black students could get an excellent education. The Institute's goal was to train black students to become teachers. With hard work, Addy could have earned a spot at the I.C.Y. and gone on to teach other black students in the North. After the war ended, Addy could even have gone back to the South to share her love of learning with newly freed slaves.

Read more of ADDY'S stories,

available from booksellers and at *americangirl.com*

⊙ *Classics* ⊙

Addy's classic series, now in two volumes:

Volume 1:
Finding Freedom

In the midst of the Civil War, Addy and her mother risk everything to make a daring escape to freedom in the North.

Volume 2:
A Heart Full of Hope

As Addy and Momma make a new life in Philadelphia, they find that freedom brings new changes—and has great costs.

⊙ *Journey in Time* ⊙

Travel back in time—and spend a day with Addy!

A New Beginning

Discover what Addy's life was like during the Civil War. Outrun a slave catcher, raise money for freedmen, and help Addy find her family. Choose your own path through this multiple-ending story.

⊙ *Mysteries* ⊙

More thrilling adventures with Addy!

Shadows on Society Hill

Addy is overjoyed when Poppa's new boss invites Addy's family to live on his property in Philadelphia's elegant Society Hill neighborhood. But Addy soon discovers that their new home holds dangerous secrets—and one of them leads straight back to the North Carolina plantation she escaped only two years before.

A Sneak Peek at

Finding Freedom

An Addy Classic

Volume 1

Addy's adventures continue in the
first volume of her classic stories.

A ddy Walker woke up late on a summer's night to hear her parents whispering. She thought no more of their quiet voices than of the soft chirping of the crickets in the woods just beyond the little cabin. Often she awoke to her parents' whispering. Addy liked the sound. It made her feel safe, knowing her mother and father were close by.

A small fire glowed in the hearth as the last coals burned down from the fire Momma had used to cook supper. Usually Addy liked the warm glow of the coals in the darkness. It was the only light in the windowless cabin. But tonight it just made her hotter. Sweat crawled down her small body like ants. The stiff, dry cornhusks stuffing her pallet poked through their thin covering, sticking her. Her older brother Sam lay on his own pallet near her feet. Addy could see his dark face in the firelight and hear his regular breathing. Her baby sister Esther lay next to her. Esther's steamy breath was blowing on Addy's face. Addy loved Esther, but it was too hot to be close to her tonight. Addy tried to wiggle away from the baby. When she turned from Esther, her parents stopped talking.

"Hush, Ben," Momma said to Poppa. "I think Addy woke up."

Addy kept her eyes closed, but she could hear the rustle of cornhusks when her father got up. His feet softly crossed the dirt floor. She opened her eyes just slightly as his shadow passed over her, covering her and Esther and Sam. Addy felt protected inside of it. She wanted to ask, "Poppa, what you and Momma talking about?" But she kept her mouth shut. When her parents started talking again, she listened.

"That child asleep, Ruth," Poppa said to Momma, returning to their pallet. "She tired out. They had the children out in the fields half the day worming the tobacco plants."

"Ben, listen to me," Momma said. Her voice was serious. "I don't think we should run now. The war is gonna be over soon, and then we'll be free."

"Ruth, I've done told you before, them Union soldiers ain't nowhere near our part of North Carolina. They all the way clear on the other side of the state," Addy's father replied. "Who knows when we gonna be free?"

"But Ben, we can't lose nothing by waiting. We all

together here. That count for something," Momma argued.

"Ruth, it should count, but you know it don't. With this war, times hard. Money is real tight for the masters. A whole group of slaves was sold off the Gifford plantation because Master Gifford couldn't afford to feed and clothe them," Poppa said.

"That was Master Gifford. Master Stevens would never sell us. We work hard for him. We do everything he tell us. He need me to do sewing, and you do his carpenter work." Addy had never heard her mother speak so firmly.

"What about Sam?" Poppa went on. "I got to drag him off his pallet when the morning work horn sound. He get up grumbling about not wanting to work for the master, and he take his grumbling out into the fields. He got a hot head and a hot mouth. Sam done run off once, and now he want to go fight in the war. All he talk about is going north to fight for freedom."

Freedom. That was what her parents were talking about tonight. They were talking about the kind of freedom a slave had to run away to get.

"If Sam take off by himself a second time, we might

never see him again," Momma said in a worried whisper. "I want us all to be together."

Poppa didn't answer right away. Then he said, "Uncle Solomon told me in the field today that there's a set of railroad tracks about ten miles after the river near the Gifford place. We follow them north till they cross another set of tracks. Where they cross, there's a white house with red shutters. It's a safe house. An old white woman live there, named Miss Caroline. She gonna help us. We only got to get that far," Poppa said.

In the dark, Addy hugged Janie, the small rag doll Momma had made for her, the doll she slept with every night. Her parents' talk about running away scared her. She had never heard them talk about it before. Whenever Sam talked about escaping, they told him to hush up.

"If we get caught, Master Stevens gonna split us up for sure," Momma said, her voice shaky.

"I figure ain't nothing for sure," answered Poppa, "but we got to take our chances while we got 'em. You can't go backing out on me now."

"I'm not backing out," Momma said. She sounded cross. "I'm just scared. You want to go all the way to

Philadelphia. I ain't never been no farther than the Gifford plantation. What if we get lost from each other?"

"We gonna go together and we gonna stay together. God will watch over us. You got to believe we gonna make it north." Poppa sounded sure and strong. Addy knew he could protect them, no matter what.

"Let's just wait a little longer. When the war over, we all gonna be free. All of us right here," Momma said again.

But Poppa was firm. "I hurt when I see Addy toting heavy water buckets to the fields, or when I see her working there, bent over like a old woman. Sam already fifteen, but she a little girl, nine years old, and smart as they come. She go out in the morning, her eyes all bright and shining with hope. By night she come stumbling in here so tired, she can hardly eat. Esther still a little baby, but Addy getting beat down every day. I can't stand back and watch it no more. We can't wait for our freedom. We gonna have to take it."

Momma was quiet again. Addy wasn't thinking about the heat of the cabin, her prickly pallet, or Esther's hot breath. She was waiting for her mother's answer. None came. She heard her father rise. He went to the hearth and covered the coals with ashes.

When Addy heard him lie down, her eyes popped open, but now Addy could see nothing. There was no light in the cabin. In the thick darkness, Addy knew she had heard a secret that she must keep to herself no matter how hot it burned inside her. She could feel Esther's breath on her back. Turning to face her sister, she moved close and put her arms around her. The baby's breath did not feel too warm now. Addy was glad Esther was there on the pallet with her.

As Addy fell asleep, the only voices she could hear in the night were those of the crickets in the woods.

About the Author

DENISE LEWIS PATRICK grew up in the
town of Natchitoches, Louisiana. Lots of
relatives lived nearby, so there was always
someone watching out for her and always
someone to play with. Every week, Denise
and her brother went to the library, where
she would read and dream in the children's
room overlooking a wonderful river. She
wrote and illustrated her first book when
she was ten—she glued yellow cloth to
cardboard for the cover and sewed the pages
together on her mom's sewing machine.
Today, Denise lives in New Jersey with
her husband and four sons, but she loves
returning to her hometown and taking her
sons to all the places she enjoyed as a child.